Newcastle
Short Story Award

First published in Australia in 2020 by Hunter Writers Centre
www.hunterwriterscentre.org
Newcastle Short Story Award Anthology 2020
ISBN 978-0-6484099-9-1

Cover Photography by Shane Williams
https://strikingnewcastle.com.au
Published by Hunter Writers Centre Inc. 2020

Hunter Writers Centre
PO Box 494
The Junction
Newcastle NSW2291

info@hunterwriterscentre.org
hunterwriterscentre.org

The role of a writer is not to say what we all can say,
but what we are unable to say.

Anais Nin

Table of Contents

2020 Judges

Laura Elvery & Khalid Warsame

Foreword

I entered my first short story competition over the summer break when I was 11 years old. It was a story I'd written for the Nestlé Write Around Australia competition, and after I'd binned the Paul Jennings rip-off that my older sister rightly pointed out was a Paul Jennings rip-off, I did what I – sometimes – do best: I wrote a story in a single afternoon. It was a real tragedy: I remember a girl in a car going somewhere while clutching a photo of her dying best friend. When I was shortlisted I didn't tell anyone, totally unaware that Nathan B in my grade 7 class had also been shortlisted. Our teacher asked Nathan B to stand up and read his aloud to everyone. His story was about a man, alone in a room, who SELF-COMBUSTED!! so I knew even then that I wasn't going to stick my hand up and try to follow that. When my teacher found out I'd kept it a secret he called me a dark horse. Our shortlist prize was a writing workshop in the town public library, and a backpack stuffed with chocolate bars. The promised anthology, come to think of it now, never eventuated.

But behold, readers and writers, here is your 2020 Newcastle Short Story Award anthology. And it's a beauty. What a privilege it is to read others' words. There's me, a few months ago, reading entries late at night, wondering who this writer is and where this idea came from. (Where, in fact, did odd-bod Nathan B get his exquisite and shocking idea from?). Having entered writing competitions since I was 11, and only now beginning to judge them, it offers a real double-brain effect. The writer in me admires the writer in you. The reader in me gets to the end of a great story and looks up, going, 'Oh, yep, that is GOOD.'

And a great many of these stories are very, very good. (And stories not in this anthology are good too. Me, reading the ones that didn't quite make it, imagining a conversation with the anonymous writer where I'm able to say: This came so close. Please keep going!)

Khalid and I had an excellent time reading and judging the 2020 Newcastle Short Story Award. We found a lot of overlap in the pieces of fiction we loved. My personal longlist comprised about 100 stories, which I narrowed down to 30, a shortlist I shared with Khalid who was judging on the other side of the world, in Athens. The ones that stood out had energy, originality, and charm. The authors propelled us through with authentic dialogue, unusual turns in the plot, something simple done well, confidence, and polish.

Our winner, 'Bird Swing,' is an outstanding story about a woman working for little money deep in the beauty product world, who finds herself in a bit of a pickle. 'Bird Swing' is clever, funny, inventive, with sharp sentences and an accomplished, confident narrative voice. Second place goes to 'Clearing the Air,' the sort of story that is difficult to get right: in a very short space of time and a very limited setting, the reader gleans a whole world and its credible characters. 'Clearing the Air' is tense and compelling, told by a writer who trusts the reader to understand what has come before and will come after. And congratulations to the author of 'The Romantics,' which wins third place, for telling an elegant and charming story with a fabulous voice, in a specific time and place, and for giving the reader a layer of metaphor that serves the story perfectly.

Sincere congratulations to all who entered, and to all the writers whose work is featured here. We hope you continue to write, to read the work of others, and to look out for creative inspiration, in a single afternoon, when you see a deadline looming.

Laura Elvery
20 March 2020

Newcastle Short Story Award Sponsors

Bird Swing

Ursula Robinson-Shaw

Winner, Newcastle Short Story Award

Anna could have been a model. She could have been a model, back when models were people who got discovered. She could see herself, youthful and hot-ripe, lying down in a park, loitering at a junk store, punkly unwashed, shining irrepressibly through her own bad life. She picked under her nails, thinking of mid-90s yellow-gray plastic trays, flights to glittering elsewheres, places she could have been soaped up and fussed over, picked up and put down, where she could have freeloaded and been loved and discarded and subjected to glamorous indignities and glamorously pitied and glamorously envied.

But those luscious, callow hormones had been expensed, on mid-twenties careerism, premium-generic bars, the carrot and stick of menial pay rises. Now her old sharehouse filthlords ran ceramics businesses on Instagram. Part-time ketamine dealers posted beatifically about the art of feathering onions. And there was Anna, there but for the grace of God went Anna, sitting cross-legged in a featureless meeting room, glossy as a new car.

Sitting across from her was an old woman—the furnace manager? customer liaison officer? pickaxe representative? Old. Old like the limelight of petty hatred, shuffling too slowly down a supermarket aisle. The kind of old Anna would give up her tram seat for, and resent it. She looked like she'd been hammered with her own body, the seams of her face drooping under the hanging Edison bulbs. Anna thought of all the night creams cluttering her bathroom sink that described themselves as 'age-defying.' She did not feel defiant.

How did this happen? Anna said.

The woman shrugged. The gesture looked wrong, like a wolf under her skin. A lot can go wrong with a furnace, she said. It has its own metabolisms.

A stack of croissants lay on the raw wood table between them, flaking gently onto a rimless plate. The presence of the croissants soothed Anna, though nobody in the office ever ate them. She took a mindful breath.

There were two good things about Anna's job. The first was frontline access to chemicals that kept her well in the dewy valley of maybe-she's-born-with-it. The second was that, for the most part, she didn't have to think about the technical underbelly of business. She was at her best when reducing supply-chain inefficiencies, nipping away at excesses, the globular little leftovers of defunct industry. The poky people in R&D tinkered with formulas, which was, not to get her wrong, very important work, ensuring all the tonics and alchemies made minimal impact on their bottom line. That was what engineers and scientists had in common. They kept all the finicky underwriting, the grunts and bolts of physical reality, cloistered away from the real world of business.

Anna had been rehearsing ways to say this to the old glass rep all day, prettily arranging her microaggressions, cloaking them as shop talk and straight-shooting. She'd even practiced in the office bathroom, smiling to herself in the mirror as she whispered meticulous, unkind speeches. But now, in front of the old woman, she was quiet.

The problem had begun with some blogger, pushing a snake oil natural beauty line out of her bedroom, penning a hysterical takedown of the chemicals in the company's plastic packaging. Apparently, the chemicals mimicked human hormones and, if you believed the blogger, encouraged undesirable follicle growth. Of course, this hadn't been *proven*, it wasn't like *lead*, which they only put in lipstick these days, and which everybody knew was *fine* in small doses unless you were literally *eating the stuff*, which *yes* everybody could *agree* was *bad,* but even if it *was*, women would happily pay three hundred dollars for an eye cream made of bee venom, until some influencer shilling coconut oil told them that a Do It Yourself Face-Lift contained the same chemical byproducts as a shrinkwrapped melon. One breathless caption and, overnight, scores of loyal customers dropped out of the market like plague corpses.

Production management was a pitiless job, but Anna had that special thing: a subterranean streak of pure, professional megalomania. She was unofficially in charge of functions, and these were her peerless moments in the sun. She booked out German beer halls, catamarans, and slick, fashionable gin bars, supplying mounds of cocaine on her 45k salary in the hopes of impressing anyone.

It was at such a work party she had ruined her brilliant career. The whole office, reception included, were packed into a private room, decked out in velvet 70s junk furniture—which, retro-chic or not, only made Anna think of how disgusting the 70s must have been, an entire decade that stank like the back of a couch. She'd been cutting Tony's lines up on her cracked iPad, he berating her for failing to consider that a tiny shard from the screen could dislodge itself, become embedded in his nose, and cause a hemorrhage, when she snapped up precipitously and said, Glass. Glass packaging.

Tony smiled, his eyes half-closed, readying for a lecture. Kids were always trying to *disrupt* things—showy ideas that landed short-term investment and folded companies within a year. *Glass, Anna, would mean total overhaul, tripled production costs, adjusted formulas, label redesign.* As Tony spoke, his gaze drifting and fixating on the velvet armrest, Anna had a strange, concussive vision: of glass bottles, all their different shapes and sizes; royal green, gin-blue; jet black beads; soft, buttery-looking pebbles, worn down by years in the sea. She felt that vibrating, agitated fascination particular to children, a trance-like excitement that made her body feel brittle, like it could shatter with thrill. Plastic, with its steroidal durability, made *sense*. She understood this. She explained to Tony that she understood this: yes, plastic was cheap and adaptable and could be made new forever and ever, with no foreseeable consequences whatsoever. But think of it, Tony—and at this point, she leaned in, letting her stiff, bleached hair waft vapours in his direction—a conveyer of glass droppers, winding through their warehouse like a rope of jewels—now, Tony, *that* kind of glamour never went out of fashion. And look, she told him, racing through sentences to keep ahead of her high, increased costs could be absorbed by a healthy markup in the new essential line, which meant tweaks to the new packaging could simply be incorporated into the relaunch, which meant *adjusting* rather than *reinventing* the campaign, which meant a window of opportunity to source a new manufacturer, someone who could take a tall order on a tight turnaround, and, Tony, wasn't that her *job*? To *find solutions*? Tony nodded, still staring earnestly at the armrest, and said, you're good at your job. Anna was transported.

Glass is a venerable art, the old woman said. It is harnessed by man, not governed by him. When you bring sand in contact with fire—she made a weird, gnarled gesture—you can't control what will happen.

Isn't that your *job*, Anna said. To control what happens.

A furnace is hostile, the old woman said. It's built to burn forever. If it stops, the glass freezes in its throat. It has to run all day and night. It already makes as much as it makes.

Anna felt like she was staunching a hernia. She stumbled through a few aborted consonants before falling into silence.

Production is fixed, the old woman said gently. We can't make it faster.

From the party onwards, Anna stayed back until eight, then nine, then ten, then midnight, putting the specs together, until the vision was robust enough to bring to Tony, who was a fuckwit and a wanker but who respected a good powerpoint. By this stage, their packaging scandal had congealed into a boycott. So Tony agreed. He said, in no uncertain terms—in fact, in the exact terms—no fuck-ups.

Anna had the Social Media Officer, who had a Masters' in professional writing and was paid mostly in samples, make the announcement almost immediately. Anna usually ignored socials as something that could be managed by a trendy monkey, but that night she watched the reactions pour in with a simple, whole-body glee.

We are thrilled to announce that we will be moving all plastic packaging to glass, elevating our commitment to sustainability, luxury, and personal health.

Ever been near a glass leak? the old woman asked. It's chaos. Furnace blowing great big globs everywhere. Place full of steam. Everything shattering. People running round, panicking.

How many bottles have this problem? said Anna.

It's a nasty little defect, the old woman said. Called a bird swing. We'd have to assess each bottle with the naked eye. Can't fix it once it's formed. Have to feed everything back into the furnace. Here—she placed a small bottle on the table and pushed it toward Anna with a liver-spotted hand. Look.

It was barely visible: a fine filament of glass suspended between the bottle's inner walls, like a string of spit.

When the bottle fills with fluid, the old woman said, the bird swing shatters.

How many? Anna said.

How many defects? Hard to say, the old woman replied. Could be most of them. I wouldn't try using the samples we gave you.

So you're suggesting a total recall, Anna said, feeling hysteria rise like bile. We don't have time. It's impossible.

The old woman shrugged. Unless you want your potions filled with nasties, she said. Can't have all those lovely girls out there slicing their faces up.

Lovely girls *fall over themselves* to have their faces sliced up, Anna wanted to scream. Instead, she said, I'll have my production assistant call you in the morning, not knowing or caring if the old woman knew she did not have an assistant. She stood, the weight of a fresh and horrible reality suspended above her, and walked out of the room, straight to her cubicle, shivering as she went, the puerile image of her bottle-treasury ousted by a memory: of washing dishes on a winter evening, dunking a cold wine glass in hot water, and the glass, without a lick of pressure, giving way; pulling her hand out of the sink, watching it sprout a neat stream of blood. She'd googled. Thermal shock, it was called.

Her desk was littered with product samples, glinting suggestively beneath antique pear bulbs. She lifted one, a tiny, unlabelled amber phial, and pulled the dropper out. She squeezed the serum into the cup of her hand, looked at the viscous substance for a moment, and rubbed the soft skin of her palms together. Pulling them apart, she watched them blush, turn red, fine rivulets trickling along her lifelines. Embedded in her skin were ten, fifteen, twenty shards of glass, tiny and irregular, like raw diamonds.

Clearing the air

Kathy Prokhovnik

Second Prize

The skinny woman rapped against the wooden edge of the front door, brushing the little boy and the dog into line behind her. She peered through the dimpled glass panels, suddenly impatient to have this done with.

Lyn had watched the little procession wind its way up her driveway. At the front trotted a young dog, faltering slightly at each step to pull up the foreleg with the bandage above the paw. Next came the skinny woman, her pregnancy pushing tightly against her t-shirt, her hand stretched back to the little boy who shuffled and kicked at stones. The air was filling with heat and the leaves of the trees were turning downwards. The green haze that had built across the paddocks would be gone soon.

The skinny woman saw movement through the dimples, a wobbling shape that shifted into human form as it reached the door.

'Come in,' said Lyn, smiling rigidly, opening the door wide.

'You stay here, Jess,' the skinny woman barked at the yellow dog, and it turned to look for a shady spot, dropping down between a set of glass doors and a large pot holding a cumquat tree.

Lyn stepped out of the house, disappearing around the corner, reappearing with a dog's bowl full of water. She placed it next to the pot. The dog sniffed it then put its head back down, looking at its bandaged leg then laying its muzzle gently on top of it.

The two women moved silently into the house, Lyn leading the way, the little boy trailing behind. Lyn gestured to the kitchen table, moving some papers to the sideboard and straightening the tablecloth.

'Just sorting out some accounts,' she said. 'Have a seat,' she added, while she herself turned to the bench and turned on the kettle.

'How long have you had that dog?' she asked, as if she didn't know.

'Six weeks,' the skinny woman mumbled, wanting to be past the small talk. 'Got her from McQueen, over at the truck yard,' she added reluctantly.

'One of his dingos?'

'Yeh. Her mother's a dingo.'

'They're clever dogs,' Lyn said. 'Mooneys down the road had one for years. What happened to her leg?'

11

'Gashed it getting through some barbed wire. Had to have stitches.'
'Pricey!'
'Yep. It's the boy's dog.'
The little boy leaned against his mother, draped over her legs. 'It's too hot for that,' she said, detaching him and placing him on the floor. 'Where're your cars?'
He stretched his legs out and felt in the pockets of his too-big shorts, pulling out three scratched little cars, lining them up next to him on the floor and slowly running them back and forth in turn, as if to test they still had their wheels.
'Milk?' said Lyn and the skinny woman nodded. 'What would he like?' she asked, looking down at the boy. 'I've got cordial.'
The skinny woman nodded again, and Lyn put the mugs of tea on the table with a plate of biscuits. She poured cordial and water into a plastic cup, added a cube of ice, and put the cup down on the floor next to the boy.
'Don't spill it!' the skinny woman cautioned the boy. He put down his cars and picked up the cup, sipping and clinking the fast-melting ice against the sides.
The women looked at each other across the table. Lyn smiled.
'How are you going?' she asked. 'How's the baby?' She nodded at the skinny woman's belly keeping her at a distance from the edge of the table.
'Ok,' she responded. 'Look,' she said after a pause, her throat tightening, 'I've heard what you've been saying about Drew.'
Lyn felt the back of her neck stiffen, all the way up into her head.
'What do you mean?' she asked.
'You've been saying things. That he sits around all day when he says he's building the house. Smoking dope. You reckon he's useless. You're spreading it everywhere. It's bullshit. He's done heaps on that house.'
She looked quickly down at her boy. A steady brrrm brrrm came from the floor as the cars sped on the smooth surface.
'Deb.' Lyn stopped, then started again. 'I don't know what to say. That's not true.'
'It's none of your business,' Deb interrupted, louder. 'It's none of your business what we do. What Drew and I do.'
Brrm brrrm, and the slide of small wheels on concrete.
'I know. It's none of my business,' Lyn said, nodding. 'How would I know anyway?' she added. 'I never go down there. It's none of my business.'
The last time Lyn had dropped in on Deb it had been cold, maybe winter. Deb hadn't welcomed her, but she'd gone in anyway. There was a tarp where the roof should have been, and Deb and the boy had huddled over a one-bar heater connected by a series of cords to the one power point

in the room. Lyn had handed over some soup – Thanks for taking it! Made way too much! Freezer is full! – and got home quickly, back to her fireplace and her plump sofa and her house that kept out the wind.

'Clarrie goes down there but,' Deb snapped. 'Clarrie's down there all the time. Reckons he's 'helping'. I reckon he's snooping, wasting everyone's time.'

The little boy stood up and looked at his mother, then at the table. His eyes caught the biscuits, and his hand reached towards them.

'Ask!' his mother said.

'Please?' he said, looking at Lyn.

'Of course,' she replied, holding the plate out to him. They were only custard creams, but he took one and cradled it like a precious thing, nibbling at it, licking the crumbs as they formed along the edge.

The heat was creeping into the house, hitting the glass doors and windows and radiating inside. Lyn wanted to close the curtains and shut out the sun. Instead, she wrapped her hands around the mug of tea.

'Clarrie takes stuff down to Drew when he finds it. Building materials. He's always picking up offcuts down at the tip shop. Boxes of tiles. He found a nice door the other day.'

'We don't need that crap. We don't need crap from the tip. What do you think we are? Another rubbish dump?' Deb twisted in her seat, looked down at the boy holding the last corner of his biscuit.

'He only takes good stuff,' Lyn replied, tired of this conversation now, wishing she could just say – 'It's not me! It's everyone in town. We all know what's happening.' This wasn't clearing the air at all. That's what Deb had said. Let's clear the air. The air was just filling with sharp splinters of accusation. 'We used stuff from the tip ourselves when we were building here,' she added, her voice wearing out as she said it.

The two women looked at each other. Lyn shifted her gaze first, searching the room for comfort, looking for support in the photos of her children on the wall, all three of them beaming out from under graduates' caps. If only she could find the right thing to say. But then, why did she care about this woman and her boy and her unborn child and her stupid husband who was running her into the ground while he sat around pretending to build them a house that would never be finished. There were limits to neighbourliness. He'd go off and leave her one day, leave her in a house with no bathroom and a tap outside the back door where she'd have to fill buckets to bathe the baby and do the washing up. Then Lyn would be stuck, like last time, trying to find ways of helping that Deb wouldn't bristle at – a loaf of bread she bought by mistake, a surplus of beans from the garden.

The little boy stood up and reached for another biscuit.

'No more!' his mother snapped. 'We're going home.'

She stood to leave, and Lyn rose too. 'Please don't go,' she said, wondering why the words were coming from her mouth. 'Please, let's clear the air.'

Deb stared at her, felt the pull of sympathy, an unreliable basis for anything.

Before she could reply, a low growl came from the dog outside. Both women turned to look. Through the glass doors they could see the dog standing up slowly, the dark fur along the ridge of her back rising, her head focused on something beyond the pot. Both women quickly moved towards the doors. The dog kept its gaze fixed as the head of a brown snake appeared, with the rest of the body swiftly following. It was big. Well over a metre long, its body as thick as a child's arm, its small head darting. It was a pale one, almost pink.

'That's the one I saw yesterday,' Lyn said quietly. 'Don't worry. It was more scared of me than anything. It turned tail when it saw me in the garden.'

But as the snake's head hit the glass of the double doors and its body curved up against the surface, they heard the front door slam. Outside, the little boy was running, yelling. 'Snake! Jess! Come 'ere!' The dog switched its gaze to the boy then back to the snake. Her pose widened and she started to bark. The snake turned too, to stare at the dog. Lyn watched, paralysed by the scene unfolding on the other side of the glass – the snake whipping around to face the dog, the dog confronting the snake, legs spread, pouncing forward and back, the little boy rushing to grab the dog, the snake rearing up and then Deb was there behind the boy, pulling him backwards and screaming, 'Jess! Away!'. Then Lyn was out there too in the beating sun, taking the sobbing boy from Deb and bringing him kicking back into the house, watching Deb catch the scruff of the dog's neck and pull her towards the front door.

'Bring her in!' Lyn shouted, holding the door open with the boy on her hip, and Deb rushed in with the growling dog in her arms, keeping its flailing head and snapping mouth away from her face.

They watched the snake coil and crash against the doors, as if it could melt right through into the house and corner them all there. Three times they watched it weave its way along the length of the doors, gaining some sort of traction on the smooth glass, slithering up and dropping back down, its movements losing momentum until it finally fell off and glided away.

The women, the boy and the dog sat on the floor together, the heat of the sun pounding them, its glare in their eyes. The boy crawled off Lyn's lap and into his mother's. Deb loosened her grip on the dog, and it dropped to the floor with its head on its bandaged leg.

Lyn looked out through the glass doors. They retained something of the menace of snake, even though they were empty of its writhing. She looked beyond to the garden, bleaching in the full sun, to the zucchini leaves wilted like unfurled umbrellas, and the tomatoes that had been turning red yellowing instead.

'Are you ok?' Lyn asked, looking at Deb, stretching out a hand. She saw her splayed legs, cheap sandals with broken straps, toes falling out. A protruding belly, arms cradling the limp boy. She saw her face relax and quiver, her eyes screw up, her mouth fall open. She saw the sheer exhaustion of someone who tries to pretend her fears won't be realised.

Deb opened her eyes. 'Yep,' she said. 'I'm baking here,' she said, standing the boy up and pushing herself up from the floor. Lyn stood and held out her hand again. Deb reached up and took it, felt the dampness of her own hand in its strong grip, and let herself be helped up.

The Romantics

Margaret Hickey

Third Prize

By the mid-90s, my friends and I are burnt out and in various states of backpacker decline. Tired and ill from too many nights drinking and dancing, we resign ourselves to getting some rest and making some cash. Rumours reach our country town in Australia that hint at us turning wild; anxious parents take long flights to issue threats. The act is a wake-up call, we scatter across the globe.

I sign up to a job agency in London, looking after old people. I say I'm willing to go anywhere that doesn't involve a flight. That same afternoon, I get a job looking after an elderly woman near Penshurst in Kent. It's for two weeks only and I resign myself to boredom. The quiet nights will do me good. I sleep the whole way there.

When I first meet her, Lady Jane is in her wheelchair, waiting. She has a tartan blanket over her lap and a string of pearls about her neck. She is wearing a purple jumper with a white shirt and her mauve skirt is long and pleated. Behind her; a manor house three storeys high and acres of landscaped grounds. Lady Jane asks if I'm named after the Queen's sister. I say no, my aunt. The old Lady tutts, turns her wheelchair around and I think, this is not going to end well.

The first few days are long and lonely. I help Lady Jane get dressed, I cook her meals, I assist her in the shower. A nurse comes once a day. At night, I lie in my single bed with thick cotton sheets and I listen to the big old clock, given to her by some cousin of the Queen going tick, tock, tick, tock. I'm used to stumbling home drunk and sleeping with my friends in the same room. Or having chats to someone in the bunk above or below. It's so quiet in the manor house. Old nightmares threaten, I fight them and mostly win.

On my breaks, I walk. At first around the manor house and then beyond, through green fields and woods of oak and dappled shade. I pass through kissing gates and follow little paths and bridleways. Sometimes I cry when I walk through the old forests and I'm not entirely sure why. Every step is a poem.

Lady Jane watches me from her window and on my return, I take to recounting my walks. We bend in close, we pore over maps, we plot new routes. Over rambles, we bond. Lady Jane tells me of other, secret places that she used to go when she was younger. At her urging, I enter deeper in the woods to a place of twisted trees, where an old wooden bridge lies broken over the river. I lie down with my cheek on moss and think it's worth it to take untrodden paths. I grow stronger. At night, we read poetry. We like Coleridge and Wordsworth, Eliot and Keats. Shelley too. I read her Clancy of the Overflow and she agrees it's up there. Lady Jane can be confused; once, she slapped me lightly on the face and said, 'Ethel, you're becoming a bore!'

When I wash her silver hair, Lady Jane tells me stories. She's only ever had one lover and they kissed just once on Hastings Beach before he left for war. She never saw him again. When I ask if she loved him, she says that she thinks she did and perhaps more with time.

I'm 24 and I've only told one person I loved them and it wasn't my family or the boy I went out with for a year. A memory: My friends and I are on the tube in peak hour. Londoners sit like dignified tombstones, we are colourful bats lining the side. I'm wondering aloud what line Kilburn is on and a young man in a suit, not much older than us says, It's this one, and I say thank you and then I say, good book because he's reading *Far from the Madding Crowd* and he says have you read it and I say, I have. Then my friends and I nudge one another, because he really is an absolute spunk. When he alights at the next stop, my friends sing him goodbye and I call out with reckless joy, I love you! and he turns and calls back, I love you too! and the Londoners in the train smile into their laps and we in the carriage are carried in a warm glow all the way to Kilburn.

Back in Kent, I ring the agency and tell them I'd like to stay on. Weeks turn to a month, then two, and when a car pulls up with niece and grand-nephew, it feels like a rude intrusion.

The niece is a snob and the son, perhaps 20, talks only of stocks and property. He is still in thrall to his school and likes to mention parades and raucous dinners. He tells me all this when he's followed me on one of my walks. I find a massive leaf in the shade of an old oak. I say I'm going to use it as a pillow and he says that I am very strange. I take him to the river and throw a rock in the water beside him. He jumps about, offended and wet. I suggest he throw a rock in beside me to make it even, but he refuses and walks across the field in a huff. Ethel, you're becoming a bore.

The next day, Lady Jane is in a jumpy, excited state. She wants us to go to Pevensey Beach for a picnic. The niece and I eye each other across the room. It is a terrible day, grey and windy with rain. But Lady Jane won't be dissuaded, we pack our thermoses, we drive to Pevensey beach.

Once there, we sit hunched on pebbles and look out to mutinous waves. Lady Jane brings up the fact that I used to be a lifeguard. I deeply regret telling her this.

'At a pool!' I say, 'not the ocean.'

Lady Jane says that I should go for a swim and that Australian girls are very strong and hardy.

'No one would swim in that,' the niece says.

'An Australian girl would!' Lady Jane says and I close my eyes.

'No one would,' the niece snaps her purse shut and pulls her scarf around her neck.

Before I can change my mind, I'm kicking off my shoes and pulling my jeans down. I tear off my jacket and lift my jumper and long sleeve top over my head. The wind eats into me as I run across the pebbles and into the sea.

It's the worst agony I've ever experienced. My limbs freeze up and I forget to breathe. When the water hits my stomach, I scream. Teeth explode in my head when I dive under. My head shrinks. Purgatory is ice, not fire. I try to dive under once more but cannot. I turn and run as best as I can back up the beach to the little party, sitting now with open mouths.

The son asks, 'how was it?' and I reply, 'cold at first, but lovely once you're in'.

When I reach down to pick up the blanket he offers, the son touches the crook of my elbow, rubs his warm fingers there lightly for just a second.

'I thought your skin would be rougher' he says in a kind of wonder.

I flick the blanket up toward me and throw it about my shoulders, but not before I see a mother's dark look.

On the way home in the car with my head still aching– Lady Jane talks of poetry. I sit in the front passenger seat, listening to her try to recount the Ancient Mariner. Inspired by the sea, she wishes to hear it. She prods my arm, asking for help and after a moment I recite it – the whole first part of the poem. My jaw warms up with the recital. Blood surges through my frozen limbs, I come to life. The rest of the party is quiet.

'Why on earth would you know that?' The mother asks.

I eye her through the rear vision mirror. 'Honours in English Literature, First class.'

'Impressive,' nephew says.

His mother sits back in the seat, sniffs. 'The accent grates,' she says, and in that moment, I decide to sleep with her son.

On the rest of the way home I let the blanket droop down low over my bare shoulder, displaying for all the distinct lack of tan-lines.

I steal into his room that night and slide in between the covers. He's wearing pyjamas and reading Clive Cussler.

'Do you come here often?' I ask.

'I haven't slept with many girls,' he says, which I take to mean none and his hands shake like a young leaf.

His mother in the room next door calls, 'How are you getting on in that hard-old bed darling?'

He shouts back, 'Perfectly well I believe,' and we laugh and laugh into the pillows.

After, we have a cup of tea and a hobnob. He tells me he hasn't had a girlfriend and I suggest that he should hold off on talking about his family lineage, or stocks or where he went to school. It's boring, I tell him. Girls don't care about Dads who are Viscounts.

'Some do,' he says, 'some want all that comes with it' and perhaps he is right. But not the girls I know. Not me.

'What do you want?' He asks and I tell him glow worms.

'Wordsworth,' I add, and he says ahhh. But I don't know if they taught him Wordsworth at his public school or his father's bank where he now works.

The next morning, I'm up early. I go right around the woods and past Penshurst place. I sit on top of a kissing gate and listen to the birds. The week before, one of my friends suggested in a glum voice that perhaps it was time we should start looking for boyfriends. I kick my feet against the wooden posts. Boyfriends can go to hell, I think. But the thought rests uneasy and doesn't go away.

When I get back to the manor, the visitors have gone and there's a note on my bed, lying on top of the massive leaf:

Australian girl
Doesn't like prissy blokes or stocks
Only likes trees and walks
And poetry

In years to come, a friend will send me the section of a glossy magazine where his society wedding is featured over one page. In the background, his mother scowls. I hope his wife is Australian.

When I tuck her in that evening, the night is full of silver moon. Lady Jane is 94. One kiss in all that time. In her blue night dress, lying in her narrow bed, Lady Jane looks tiny. She touches the side of my face with her thin hand and I press my cheek on hers. I think; she's not long for this world.

In my bedroom I look out toward the twisted trees and admit that Kent has made me a romantic. Six months ago, I would have cried for Lady Jane and fretted over her lost love. Now, I see glimmering lights everywhere I look.

Perhaps that that one kiss of Lady Jane's was worth it, worth all the drunken, glorious trysts I have had. Perhaps it was the kiss to end all kisses, 'when soul meets soul on lover's lips' as Shelley wrote. You could live on such a kiss for fifty years or more, it would fill whole days and restless nights.

A kiss on the beach, a letter on a leaf, a declaration from a train.

Like glow worms on a cold English night, we are lifted up, carried along and placed.

We burst and fade, we burst and fade.

Future Proof

George McElroy

Highly Commended

Graham is deciding whether to leave me or not. He's been chewing it over for the past couple of weeks. He shuffles around the house, opening doors to different rooms, standing in the doorway, then closing the door again. Over breakfast, pouring milk onto his Weet-Bix, he says things like *I just don't know if there is enough here* and *What if there is someone out there I really click with?*

He always was a think-out-loud type of guy.

I want to help him out, I really do. I hate seeing him locked in this indecision. But this morning, the timing is not good. I have the phone on my ear with Deb crying on the other end. I put my hand over the receiver and I say to him, 'Can we do this later?'

There's been another break-in at the shop. It's the third time this month.

'The little shits,' Deb says, between sobs. She takes this kind of thing to heart. I'm paying her minimum wage; she needn't get so emotionally entangled.

'It's ok,' I soothe her. 'Never mind.'

Not much has been taken: two hundred dollars, the float amount. But they've also walked out with the cash register.

'Did you lock up last night?' Deb asks me. 'Because it doesn't look like it.'

I hesitate for a second. 'Yes,' I say. I think I did. I'm pretty sure I did.

'Damn it, Lucy,' she says. 'You're hopeless.'

It's unsettling, the recent spate of burglaries. We'd always assumed we were immune to random acts of crime, being a small town where everyone knows everyone. Deb's neighbour, Maria, was hit first. The thieves snuck in and pocketed half a packet of TimTams and some homemade date slice. Maria came into the shop that morning terribly shaken up. The thing is, not many of us lock our doors. Even if we had the inclination, most doors do not have a lock. Maria said she'd lived in town for thirty years and never

23

ever had she considered locking her door.

Deb sat Maria down, feet up on a chair, and brought her a strong hot tea.

'Throw out your toothbrush,' she said. 'That's the first thing they do. They take your toothbrush and scrape it around the toilet bowl.' She'd seen this on a documentary about crime.

Deb has a lot of good advice to dole out. She has firm rules about what to eat and what to wear. She never touches sausages or any kind of processed meat. Sometimes at lunch she'll eat a plain cheese sandwich on white bread. That way, if any food gets stuck in her teeth, it's inconspicuous. She'll never be seen in tracksuit pants in public. Her biggest fear is having someone visit her at home unexpectedly and catch her in tracksuit pants. I tell her there are probably worse things that could happen, but she looks dubious. Deb thinks I'm careless.

When I get down to the shop the police van pulls up beside me. We walk in together to face Deb. As usual the cops can't do much. Townsfolk have a hunch about who is responsible, but no proof. These are sweet-tooth thieves, with a penchant for Mars Bars and Coca Cola. The police shrug and put their hands out to the side in a 'don't shoot' gesture. They do this to Deb, who's getting all worked up again, waving a spatula around as she speaks.

'Don't leave cash on the premises,' they say in a reprimanding tone, as if they've told me before. They have, in fact, told me before.

'I always tell her that,' Deb says. 'She's hopeless.'

'And I'd really consider an alarm. Plus CCTV. This is becoming a pretty common occurrence.' Their eyes travel over the saggy building. There are, their eyes seem to say, things you can do to stop the rot.

I put the alarm on my to-do list, which is steadily growing. On the list: install security alarm and cameras, purchase new cash register, help Graham decide whether to leave me or not, get television fixed.

Fixing the television is something Graham could do. I suspect all the doubts have arisen because he has too much time on his hands. With no harvest this year, he hasn't landed the usual work at the grain silos. All over the district, money and work has dried up with the drought. And with the television broken, he's been overthinking things. It's his tendency. Deb wouldn't leave that temptation open to a man, not if she wanted to keep him. She'd have him cleaning gutters, changing washers on the taps. There would be no time for indecision in Deb's house.

At the hardware store, the sales assistant finds me in the security systems aisle.

'You need help,' he says.

'Yes,' I concede.

I open my mouth to speak, but instead I start to cry. I didn't anticipate such insight from the guy. Or maybe he's just doing his job. Either way, now big fat tears roll down my face and plop audibly on my shoes. The sales assistant emits soothing throat noises to accompany my tears.

'It's not how I ever wanted to live. Like this,' I say. I wave my hand along the length of security devices. 'My shop is such a little shop,' I add.

The sales assistant puts his finger on his chin. 'Here's the thing,' he says. 'We all want to live in a world where we can trust people. Am I right?'

I nod.

'So this is about respect.' He lifts a camera off the shelf. 'This is about deterrence. That's all. Don't think of it as spying. It's about training people to act normal, to act nice. Let me show you something.'

He leads me to the back of the store, taps some buttons on a keyboard and spins a computer monitor to face me. It's me in the aisle. Oh, God. I look wretched. Also, I need a haircut.

'See,' he says. 'Doing nothing wrong. Nothing to see here. All you're going to do is make people behave better. You ask me, that's a good thing. That's a no-brainer.'

Last week I told Graham to get an A4 piece of paper and make two columns: pros and cons. This could be helpful, I said, in the decision-making process. He brightened up considerably when I suggested that. Another time I just snapped at him: 'I wish you'd make up your mind for once in your life.' I didn't mean to sound so harsh. His indecision is one of the qualities that drew me to him. He looked reproachfully at me then.

'But how do you know?' he said. 'How do you ever really know?'

The cash register is sighted, minus cash, in the government dam on the town outskirts. It doesn't float to the surface like some bloated dead body. Cash registers don't float, dead or alive. It's just with the prolonged drought the dam is a muddy puddle, and cash registers don't throw too far. Needless to say, the cash register cannot be salvaged.

The town kids wander in after school to order their Chiko Rolls and hot chips. They drape their bodies over the counter.

'What do you know?' They drawl.

Deb chases them out with the tongs.

I try to remonstrate with her. 'There's no need for that,' I say. But she's unmoved.

There really isn't any need, since the man from the hardware store has been to install cameras inside and outside the shop. He stood on a wobbly ladder, sweat blooming under his sleeves, as Deb glared at him.

The kids are unfazed. They wait out on the street for their food. I suspect they like Deb better for this: the clear demarcations.

At the pub they hold a drought-relief night. All proceeds from the sausage sizzle will go to help struggling farming families. It's to bring the community together. In the bar, people cluster along lines which seem more impenetrable each year. The publican is shaking his head at one of the townies who has walked into the bar. 'No more credit,' he is saying. He puts his hands up and shrugs his shoulders.

I take a sip of something which is in my left hand, the stubby Graham placed there before making his way to the loo. It tastes like mud.

'I'm done in,' I say to Graham when he returns to take his beer.

'We only just got here,' he says.

But I need to go. 'See you at home,' I say.

At the house, I reach for my keys in my pocket. The keys aren't there, and neither is my pocket, and I realise I've left my coat on a plastic chair in the beer garden. My phone too. 'Damn it, Lucy.' Deb's voice echoes in my head. I walk back to the pub. Inside the bar, a local woman blocks my path.

'It's common knowledge,' she says, looking at me with one eyebrow raised. 'You with me?'

I shake my head. I scan the bar for Graham, but he's not anywhere I can see. The woman leans in.

'Until they're caught red-handed the cops won't do a thing about it. Bloody hopeless,' she says. She pats my hand, and hiccups. I don't know if she means me, or the police, or it's just a comment on life in general.

Out back, in the beer garden, it's deserted. But then I detect movement in a dark corner, and two figures in the process of disentangling. The larger figure darts into a nearby oleander bush. The smaller figure, I discover, is Deb.

'Lucy?' she says, in a very non-Deb tone of voice, in a tone lacking any kind of certainty. In a tone suggesting she has been caught in a compromising position. Then she smiles at me, which is peculiar. Deb is not a person given to smiles.

I move closer.

'What's that stuck in your teeth?' I say.

She snaps her lips shut.

It's sausage, that's what it is. It's the sausage in bread she ate earlier, a flagrant violation of her own rules. Hell. So much for the life advice.

'You can come out,' I say to the man crouching in the oleander bush.

He comes out. I breathe. It's not Graham. Not that I truly believed it was Graham, only fleetingly considered it might be Graham. But no, the person in the oleander bush is the hardware man.

'You!' I say. I turn to Deb.

'What?' she says. She moves to the hardware man and straightens his collar, brushes a leaf off his sleeve. He is grinning foolishly, one hand busily pushing his hair over towards his right ear, again and again.

'How's the security system working out for you?' He says.

I bump into Graham as I go back inside the bar and we make accidental eye contact. It feels like a long time since we've done that: looked at one another.

'Come home?' I say.

He has to think about it. He looks down at his half-drunk beer and over his shoulder.

'Yeah ok,' he says.

We cross the road in front of the shop. Under the awning, the security camera gleams, catching the reflection of the streetlights. I don't know why I do this, but I bend down and select a smooth grey stone from the roadside, where the asphalt gives way to dusty gravel. I run my thumb over the stone's surface, measure its weight in my hand. Then I take the stone and throw it, hard and straight, directly at the black eye of the camera. There is a sharp satisfying crack.

'Don't ask,' I say to Graham, and he doesn't. He takes my empty hand in his and leads me home.

Salt

Michelle Wright

Highly Commended

The sun's getting low on New Year's Day, and the last of the town kids shamble home, small arms sandy-sore from digging. The rising tide seeps into the hole they've left behind, and the sodden walls sag and crumble in

Mama Lily hobbles past, her crook leg heavy from the long afternoon of hauling washed up fishing nets off the beach. There'd only been one turtle. Long past rescuing. Sand-stuffed holes for eyes and flippers sawn to the bone.

Coming in from the east, sodden clouds smother the sky as the coconut palms lean low and rattle in the evening breeze. Mama Lily turns her head and whistles towards Thud the Staffy.

'Home, home,' she yells, yanking the handle of her esky in the crook of her right elbow. Thud stops snapping at the foam on the water's edge and runs after her as she starts the long, slow walk back towards her hut.

On the clutter of stones below the cliff, a newspaper-wrapped bundle flaps open and shut; seagulls squawking, hovering overhead. Thud runs ahead of Mama Lily, following the smell of deep-fried fish. He pushes his snout into the bundle, vacuuming up the few soggy chips still clinging to the paper. Mama Lily lumbers up, calling him away, but he doesn't come back. He circles the bundle, his mouth wide in his wacky grin, drooling as he licks up grains of salt. She whistles again, knowing that the salt will make him thirsty and that she's finished the bottle of water she brought with her. As she gets close to the newspaper, she sees that it's weighed down, full and heavy. She pushes at it with her cane.

'Holy Mother of God,' she yells as the bundle starts to cry.

Mama Lily carries the baby home in the esky, her hip-swaying gait sending it to sleep. She puts it on the kitchen table and pushes Thud's dribbling snout away.

'Quiet,' she says. 'It's sleeping.'

Mama Lily pulls the paper back. A red-faced boy, greasy still with matted, flattened hair, salt grains caught in waxy folds, the cut umbilical cord hanging to one side. He looks up at her, eyes unfocussed, frowning. Mama Lily looks back at him. She releases the breath she's been holding in.

'We're keeping him,' she says. Thud grins his wide-mouth grin and wags his tail.

Mama Lily makes a nappy from a towel cut in two and strokes the baby's tummy with her thumb. From the medicine box, she takes an eye-dropper and sterilises it in a pan of boiling water. She dilutes cow's milk with water and dissolves a spoon of sugar in it. She fills the eye-dropper with milk and slips her pinkie into the baby's mouth. When he starts sucking, she slides the eye-dropper in next to her finger and slowly squeezes tiny squirts of milk onto his tongue.

Darkness comes and Mama Lily's mangled leg begins its nightly pounding. The ache loops its way around her calf and through her thigh, then clamps around her hips. She keeps her body in constant motion, carrying the baby pressed tight to her chest, trying to keep the pain at bay; her walk a looping, swinging waltz. After the attack, the doctors had hoped the feeling might be lost, but the obstinate nerves refused to quit. They kept their tiny hooks sunk in. So now, she feels every inch of flesh and skin in her gammy leg, even though there's more of it missing than there.

It was on a New Year's Day, hot and heavy like this one was - nineteen sixty-nine. Fifty years ago today. Her left leg shredded by a tiger shark during a drunken midnight swim. She hadn't ventured far off shore, but it was lurking near the river mouth, hoping for an easy snack. After her boyfriend dragged her up onto the beach, she saw its fin heading back out to sea, satisfied no doubt by the small piece of her calf and the bigger chunk of her thigh that it had managed to gulp down. In the moonlight she could see where the attack had happened, the surface of the water swirling still, pale scraps of flesh carried by the outgoing tide, frantically nibbled at by a swarm of baitfish. Her boyfriend carried her to his car and lay her on the back seat, their beach towels soaking through with blood, wrapped tight around her leg.

At the doctor's surgery, they managed to stop the bleeding and gave her something for the pain. They said she was lucky that the major arteries were untouched. Otherwise she would have bled to death. It was mainly fat and muscle that had suffered. What survived was stitched and bandaged and, later, covered by skin grafts and left at that. When it healed, it looked like a stormy sea - big hollows and ridges, in place of gentle swells.

First thing the next morning, Mama Lily puts a towel in the bottom of the esky and lays the baby down. She covers it with a tea-cloth, slings it over her arm and makes the hour long trip by coach into Carnarvon. She goes to the chemist and buys formula, a baby bottle, nappies and a dummy. She pays no attention to the questioning look the pharmacist throws her way.

On the wire stand in front of the newsagency, the newspaper headlines talk about a young woman found half unconscious, bleeding in the dunes. Mama Lily goes inside and buys the local paper. She waits till she's alone at the bus stop before she opens the paper and starts reading. The article takes up the whole of page two. It says the young woman is not a local. She looks to be in her late teens. She's refused to give her name, refused to say where she's come from, refused to say what she did with the baby. The police are appealing for help to find the abandoned newborn. They hold grave fears for its safety.

Once Mama Lily finishes the article, she tears the whole page out and screws it tight into a ball. She throws it up onto the bus-stop roof and then waits in the shade below for the coach to come and carry them back home. She takes the dummy from its case and pulls the tea-cloth back. She slips it into the baby's mouth and watches as it starts sucking, its eyelids fluttering, then closing.

When she gets home, she goes outside to the quiet of the porch and puts her leg up on a box. The baby drinks curled into her lap, the suck and backwash of the bottle like the gentle rush of waves. She looks into his face, the blackness at the centre of his eyes. She feels the old familiar sorrow seep deep within her chest. All these years it has leaked behind her heart, a dripping tap of grief. She leans him up against her shoulder and rubs his back in circles like she'd done with her own long-gone son.

When the baby falls asleep, she holds it on her chest, its palms clenched and pushed against her windpipe. She hums and feels the vibrations pass between their bodies. She presses her lips to the top of the baby's head, tasting the warmth of the downy skin against the tip of her tongue. She draws it away and presses it to her palate. Where there should be sweetness, there's only salt. She isn't sure if it's the chips or the ocean that have left their mark, or if it's a rising to the surface of some elemental substance. She knows that, without a doubt, this baby is where it needs to be. She'll be the one to fulfil its every need. She knows what their lives will become. The taste of it is on her tongue and it won't go away.

Early afternoon, just as she puts the baby down to sleep, she sees a police car pull up in front of her place. The officer in the passenger seat stays in the car and a young female officer gets out of the driver's side. Mama Lily recognises her – Nadia. She's known her since she was a little girl. She used to come around with a gang of kids and spy on her from behind the tea-tree bushes. They were all terrified of her. Since she became a police officer fifteen years ago, she's been out to see Mama Lily hundreds of times. Mainly welfare checks to make sure she's still alive. Three or four times to follow up on a complaint.

'Hey, Lil,' says Nadia, taking off her cap. She pulls a damp strand of hair from her forehead and pushes it behind her ear. 'Heard you were in town this morning.'

Mama Lily pulls a chair out from the kitchen table and lowers herself slowly onto it. Nadia pulls out the other chair and sits down, not waiting for an invitation.

'Lil,' she says. 'Can you tell me why you bought a whole lot of baby supplies from the chemist?'

Mama Lily doesn't answer. She rubs her knuckles up and down her aching thigh. Nadia waits a few more seconds before continuing.

'There's a baby that was born about twenty-four hours ago. Its mother left it on the beach.' She knows that's where Lil spends all her time, getting rid of ghost nets, rescuing any turtles she finds alive. She leans forward until she's directly in her line of sight. 'I know you have it, Lil.'

Mama Lily runs her tongue across her teeth before she speaks. 'It's a he,' she says. 'And I've given him a name.'

'Okay,' says Nadia. 'What have you called him?'

'Alfie,' she replies. Mama Lily looks away and rubs her thumb across her eyelid. 'What'll happen to him?' she asks.

'I imagine he'll be put up for adoption,' says Nadia. 'There's lots of families desperate for a baby.'

Mama Lily looks down at the floor, the gaps between the mismatched lino tiles filled with sooty crud.

'Fair enough,' she says, laying her palm on Thud's hot and dribbling snout. She watches through the window as Nadia carries the baby out to the car.

Later that afternoon, Mama Lily goes down to the beach. She walks all the way to the end where there's a pile of orange fishing net washed up on the sand. As she gets close, she sees that there's a turtle caught, the net slicing through one front flipper. She kneels and tries to hold it still it as she cuts through the nylon net. When it's free, she wraps her arms around it and struggles to pick it up, but it fights its way free and splashes out through the waves, its injured flipper flailing.

Mama Lily lies down in the shallow water, exhausted from the battle. The tide is coming in. With each small wave, the water washes over her throbbing leg, splashing up against her arms, small drops landing on her cheeks and lips. She rests and lets the sun dry out the drops of water. Thud sits by her side, his snout pushed up against her forearm, licking at the tracks the drops have left behind, crooked and white like dry creek beds.

Leibniz and Newton Take the Train

Andrew Roff

Commended

Haruka's nose pressed against the suit jacket of the passenger in front. She thought about Gottfried Leibniz.

It was the same each morning. Wait in the crush to board the train, northbound on the Chiyoda. During peak, the line ran at 181% of capacity. At Yushima, where Haruka joined, always there were patient queues in front of the marks indicating just where the train would stop. A stable formation, until the doors opened and the attendants began scrummaging from the back of the platform to wedge in more passengers. Haruka was proud of the efficiency.

The soap-concealed cigarette reek of the salarymen, the jostle of the train and the press of humid bodies all around her, the warmth and tightness in her chest when she inhaled dank air: some part of her was conscious of it all. But she did not give those impressions licence. They could not access the muscles that controlled her face or her hand that loosely gripped the pole. Even though it might feel otherwise, there was a vast distance between herself and the man at her back.

Haruka had been in high school when she first learned about Leibniz. The old physicist had held that without matter, there could be no void. Emptiness was only bestowed with meaning by the position of the bodies amongst it, just as love could not exist without lovers. No kinship without family. No society without citizens.

Then there was Isaac Newton, Leibniz's contemporary and great rival. Newton-sensei had disagreed most emphatically. He wrote that absence had its own existence, independent of any countervailing presence. But Haruka always thought that Leibniz's view was the more Japanese. Each bond had an anchor, each train a station, each obligation a debtor. Emptiness could only be appreciated because the universe was full. Newton was *hikikomori* in his physics: a shut-in loner.

Her parents had named her Haruka, and so she was. The character that made her name,

had a meaning of distance, remoteness. Like most children, Haruka had learned to write her name and make it beautiful, practicing brush strokes, filling scrolls with copies of herself. It was the smooth release at the end of a stroke that Haruka could not master. Perhaps Newton would have enjoyed the blank paper that remained when she packed away her calligraphy set.

The village of Haruka's childhood had seemed full, to her. Nine days after she graduated high school there was an occurrence at Fukushima, not so far away. Afterwards, the discussion continued for weeks until finally, the government announced that it was not safe to remain. There was an emptying, and Leibniz might have said that the place ceased to exist. Her parents moved north, to a seaside village in Aomori Prefecture. Haruka travelled south, to Tokyo and university. At the start of each year, her colleagues returned to their birthplaces to spend a day or two, but Haruka could not. And now she worked to prevent further dislocations of the type that had claimed her home.

Thoughts like these drew her away from the crowded train car. In minutes she would arrive at Kita-Senju, for the switch to the calm and comfort of the Tsukuba Express. At Kashiwanoha, a quick bus ride and an even shorter walk would have her at the Institute. Point to point to point. She was fortunate to have her research fellowship. Fortunate, also, that her morning commute was not too long by Tokyo standards.

The day began to unspool as soon as she arrived, predictable with great certainty. She greeted the space, turning on lights and checking the status of the corrosion test loop that had been left to run overnight. Half an hour later, Sato-sensei bustled in with his briefcase. Haruka followed him into his office and delivered an update. After that, she took her seat at the workstation near the stairwell, and continued verifying datasets that had been supplied by an American facility. The Americans, too, were developing a molecular trap for minor actinide extraction. It would be to everyone's benefit if their findings could be shown to match those of the Institute.

Through the glass window of his office, Haruka could see Sato-sensei typing. She didn't know much about her supervisor, and she assumed there was not all that much to know. He was in his fifties, with a mop of greying hair that was too long and unruly to allow anyone to mistake him for a regular salaryman. He had a wife and a child, a little boy. He had a car—a Honda. On his desk, there was a photograph of Sato-sensei clasping hands with Asimo, the famous robot. Sato's hobby was baseball, but he didn't play.

At lunchtime she walked to a nearby Family Mart and purchased onigiri. Besides Sato-sensei, the clerk at the store was the only person she would speak to that day. It was a fine autumn afternoon, not too humid, and she took her lunch to the municipal park and found a bench next to the rose garden. A Tuesday, so the local police orchestra was practising in the amphitheatre nearby. Recently they had taken to ending their sessions with a rendition of *What a Wonderful World*.

Haruka felt a momentary pang about buying her food. She could have risen earlier and cooked her own lunch—a bento that would have been prepared with greater consideration. But academics didn't care too much about those things, and most of her colleagues without wives did the same as Haruka and purchased their lunch from a *kombini*, or from one of the vendors lining the arcades that fed off the subway tunnels.

She studied the triangular shape of the rice ball, wrapped tightly in nori. Onigiri was an elegant method of containment: a core of fish or meat insulated by sticky white grains, and shielded by nori. Haruka took small bites, registering the savoury flavour of the seaweed.

Tokyo had slow, cool bubbles dotted through the concrete, like the park in which she sat, and for the most part Haruka enjoyed living here. Had she followed her parents north, she would have needed to find a job as an office lady. Now that she was in her late twenties, people would have started referring to her as a Christmas cake, meaning that she was sitting on the shelf, growing stale. Her parents would feel obliged to send her on arranged group dates with other young people. But here, no one bothered her, and there were plenty of women who delayed.

Sometimes on the weekends, when she had a spare afternoon, she would read visual novels on her computer. The ones made for women, typically concerning a high school student trying to win the affections of one of the popular boys. At critical moments during the story, the reader was presented with options for how the protagonist should respond.

Haruka didn't exactly read these tales for the romance. And the sex was usually not as graphic as in the versions written for *otaku*—although there were exceptions. What she most enjoyed was the finite number of choices the reader was offered to direct the story. In a given instalment, there might be 14 possible endings, and once all permutations had been explored, it was possible to perfectly control the main character's destiny. This felt like as much choice as a person could want.

As for Haruka, she knew what was expected of a wife, and she could guess at the costs and benefits. The way she lived now, there was no time for such things. Science gave her what she needed.

After lunch, she took an hour to read. Haruka found this painstaking, since most of the literature in her field was yet to be translated into Japanese. The mouth in her mind was the wrong shape, and it stumbled over names like Bruce Moyer, Alexander Ivanov, Vyacheslav Bryantsev, not to mention Einstein, and of course, Leibniz. She spent her days thinking about the efficient disposal and containment of americium, europium. There was no such thing as nipponium. Or if there was, it was yet to be discovered and named.

The late afternoon and evening were for writing up the results of Sato-sensei's investigations. Her supervisor was hopeful that this year he would have something to announce, a contribution that would reflect well on the Institute. For that to happen, their work—his and Haruka's—needed to be entirely free from error. The reputation of Japanese nuclear science had been severely damaged by the disaster, and even more so by the subsequent findings regarding TEPCO's lapses in judgment. Whatever they delivered would not only have to advance the field, it must be incontrovertible.

When she had been at the lab for about fourteen hours, Sato-sensei pushed back his chair and collected his things. As he emerged from his office, Haruka swallowed. In her loudest, clearest voice, only slightly hindered by disuse, she called to him. *O-tsukaresama deshita*—you must be tired.

Once he had left, she set about powering down the machines and locking up. She enjoyed this time, and the small rituals of departure. She double-checked the settings on the loop to ensure she hadn't overlooked anything, but even so there was a moment of uncertainty, like cresting a hill, as she pulled the lab door shut behind her. Even when taking care, people were unreliable, and it was in moments such as these that she felt her humanity.

That night she was lucky, and she walked onto the platform a few minutes before the 11:37pm semi-express. When the train arrived, she found a carriage that was almost empty, with a pair of crumple-shirted office workers nodding off down the far end. But Haruka was not alone. Leibniz was with her once more, commenting on the ambient temperature and, notwithstanding the apparent stillness of the air, describing all of the particles jiggling and crashing around their heads. A few seats further down, Newton sat sullenly, inspecting his puffy fingers and chewing his lip.

When Leibniz spoke Japanese, it was with a thick Teutonic accent He occasionally spoke to her in German, too, or some pidgin language that sounded to Haruka like German, imploring her to understand something, perhaps something about her work. But at those moments she couldn't comprehend him. Naturally she couldn't—she was aware that this version of Leibniz was a product of her own mind, and she could not gift herself understanding so easily.

Yushima station rushed at the train, enveloping her carriage on all sides, and deceleration tugged at her centre of gravity. The usual announcement was made, and the doors parted with a hiss. Silently she mouthed a goodbye as she stepped off, exiting like the last drop of liquid from an empty cup.

She encountered no one on her walk home. When she had climbed the four flights of stairs to her apartment and let herself in, she stopped to listen. It was as quiet as this city ever became. She freed her hair from her ponytail and placed her bag on its shelf in the entryway.

Every day, at the beginning and the end, this was what remained: Haruka's tiny mansion. In the main room she could spread her arms wide without touching a wall. It was immense, beyond all understanding or ease.

Fishery

Jo Langdon

Commended

He loses her just like that, stupid really, the words thrown out in someone else's voice, feels like, as the group of them drift—hover and turn—past the plaza's fish shop, where bright shades of flesh shine on gleaming ice beds: coral of salmon and peach curls of prawn, sprawl of flathead tails, and those great whole fish, complete with their heads—eyes, faces—the colour of dam water, then others darker and brighter at once: scales like a petrol spill.

Not the sight, though, but the damp salt-rot smell that brings up a kind of punchline, the timing irresistible, and so he calls out—to the others more than to her, though she's the one he addresses:

Hey, Desiree—close your legs, your breath stinks!

Her smile floats past him and, even though on the surface she's cool, he can tell already from her gaze how she'll cut him loose, and so he thinks, *bitch.* She doesn't have to be such a bitch when it's a joke.

They'd known each other already, prior to high school; had done French classes together in the same primary classroom, years before, listening to audio clips in which there was a character called Desiree, whom the other characters teased, called *Désolée* in mock confusion because she was clumsy—was always switching between introductions and apologies, an almost-pun: *Je suis Desiree/Oh, je suis désolée!* as she crashed into some monsieur or trod on somebody's foot or knocked over a chair. Sometimes this recorded Desiree would wail in exasperation back at the other characters: *non, non, non: je m'appelle Desiree!*

But the real Desiree had never been clumsy—she'd always been light and quick on her feet, quicker than most kids on the playground and sports courts and at athletics days. The joke hadn't been that funny to begin with, let alone any funnier transported to the yard during breaks, and probably that was what had irritated Desiree, because she could be funny, too.

Even now as it registers that *Je suis Desiree/Je suis désolée!* is a different joke, different register to what he's said now—different in its power, its stakes, he *gets it*—he feels defiant, and then she confirms his ready anger.

Go fuck yourself, she says to him across the plaza floor, and she gets the words pitch perfect—each syllable evenly weighted, but not too heavy, too loud: the words are a succession of raindrops hitting a body of water.

The flick of her head—the swinging shift of her lemon-bright hair in its plastic clasp, hair he knows to be cool and slippery felt loose between his fingers—is a quick shimmer as she turns away from him, away from them all, and if the others laughed much or at all at the crack he's missed it, but they smirk now at her rejoinder, then quickly lose interest again.

He sinks his hands into the pockets of his shorts; knows he should laugh it off, that he deserves it anyway. Still he thinks: *humourless cunt.*

For a second she feels such acute contempt for him, for them all—regardless or even more so because of what she's had with him, done with him; what they might be. The way he can shift in and out of himself this way, so that even physically he feels and looks to her like someone else now; some stupid stranger she's keen to veer away from.

She peels away from them all, this group of guys from school, and leaves the plaza, walking down to the foreshore, towards the pavilion and the shark-proof sea bath where, at the farthest-away middle of the encircling jetty, she can drop her schoolbag, peel off her socks and T-bars and turn her back—sit facing away from the diving tower and the safely bound swimmers, the gaze of the on-duty lifeguards, and look out at the bay and its horizon of granite ridges, industrial chimneys.

That it's neither personal nor true, that he would have said it to any of the girls in their group, hardly matters. But her anger flickers into fatigue; she's so bored by all of them with their bravado and their crude, vivid euphemisms—that they can say *meat wallet*, or *bean* and *flaps* or *curtains*, with their shit-eating grins, but don't have the language or fortitude for words like *clitoris* or *labia*, nor the imagination for any new, sharper synonyms; that they can't remake any words for themselves. That none of them have real guts or smarts.

Those who have touched her there, with their careless, clueless fingers or mouths, haven't known how to, or how to do it well, anyway—even when she's guided them with her words and hands. None have drawn from her any true ripples of pleasure let alone the full-bodied waves of release she can produce herself—or has had, just once so far, with one of the girls at the school a suburb from theirs.

(Never again, Desiree decides, will she kiss another woman for the benefit of any of those dickheads who like to watch girls kiss. Only for mutual pleasure, in reciprocity.)

The thought of what she might throw back at him or any of them bores her, too—the taunts too easy to summon: cocks the size and shape of acorns; the way some of them have spilled themselves across her legs or torso, suddenly wet and soft too soon, but she's always been kind and patient and easy about it. *Don't stress, do you think I care? It's only sex, just bodies, right?*

Despite the advertisements that have drifted across her awareness, for intimate washes that smell *peachy*, or the articles exhorting the insertion of jade eggs, the use of steam, Desiree hasn't spent much time worrying that her body stinks, or that its smells are wrong—but she'd like it to, like them to be, she decides now; some days she'd like to be positively monstrous, and like to reek.

Desiree has read some of her sister, Angela's university essays, anticipating the language to come—the conversations she wants to step into already, to steep herself in, however pretentious this makes her; whatever kind of a snob. There is Hélène Cixous's 'Le Rire de la Méduse,' her favourite so far by far: 'You only have to look at the Medusa straight on to see her,' says Cixous. 'And she's not deadly. She's beautiful and she's laughing.'

But also deadly, thinks Desiree. She likes that the Medusa is deadly. The words are electric in French, too, though her French is awkward, unpracticed. Angela's is closer to something of fluency and grace; is good enough that she can watch French films now without subtitles.

The last of the late-afternoon's heat is hitting her thighs and she parts them, lets the light fall onto the soft skin on the insides of her legs, hitching up the blue and grey gingham of her school dress. She'd like to feel transformed like this, to feel the skin of her legs thickening, a cool wet crust of scales rising, inexplicably in the sun's warmth, to the surface of her thighs, and her legs fusing to the ankle bone—the strength of her muscles consolidated, remade.

When she shifts her bum off the edge of the promenade planks, pushing herself away with her hands and heels, it is not an artful dive, but the plunge—the shattered water she drops into brilliant with the light that disturbs the deeper water; the surging movements and the release of her body's weight into the shocking cold—comes close to something orgasmic. She pushes her head up into the air again and paddles, ungainly in her dress, her wet hair slipping down from its clasp.

If she kicks out farther from the pier, she knows, there will be jellyfish—frightfully beautiful and alien in their milky opacity. Closer to shore is seaweed that will sweep across her arms and legs, hands and feet, like skin or hairs—coarse and slimy at once. For now it's enough to tread water, to take in the afternoon with all her senses: the rasping gulls turning overhead; the lapping sea and the way it seems to find her pulse; its smells particular to the slow tides of the bay.

Paper Cranes

Camha Pham

Commended

The glossy scallop seashell sat in the display case under the white light, fanned out, as if sunbaking on its own private stretch of beach, its undulating ridges like soft pink sand dunes.

Ella squinted, her eyes flickering across to the sign on the top right-hand corner of the glass case.

SEASHELL
He gave me this shell on the day he proposed. Thirty years later,
I found out he had been cheating on me with his receptionist
throughout the entirety of our marriage.

Ella's stomach tightened and she instinctively bit the inside of her cheek, determined to crush the swell of tears that threatened to break. She had been doing a lot of crying lately, alone in her new apartment, a one-bedroom city rental in another mass-produced concrete high-rise that had been plonked in the middle of the city's zigzagged skyline. Earlier that evening, as she lay sprawled on her couch, the drab grey walls had seemedto close in on her, inch by inch. She left her apartment in a rush, grabbing only her keys as she fled out the door.

She sensed someone at her side and shuffled over to give the person more room. It was a young woman wearing a colourful polka-dotted raincoat, her dark slicked-back hair speckled with fine beads of rain. Ella avoided the temptation to reach out and finger the sparkling baubles, instead runninga hand through her own damp hair and brushing back the wet tendrils matted to her forehead. She felt like she was on exhibit in the gallery with her puffy eyes and yesterday's sweater on, and had only come in to seek shelter from the rain after glimpsing the words THE MUSEUM OF BROKEN RELATIONSHIPS spelled out in red neon lights on the gallery window. She wasn't one to entertain the idea of fate, but this had seemed like a serendipitous moment. At the very least, she had been intrigued.

The woman next to her leaned over to read the inscription, shook her head and muttered 'Arsehole,' before wandering over to the next display case. Ella took a deep breath and walked in the opposite direction.

The Museum of Broken Relationships, she had discovered when she entered the gallery, was a travelling exhibition from Zagreb, a collection of miscellaneous items spawned from failed relationships. The premise had seemed kitsch, almost exploitative, a voyeuristic attempt to feed off others' heartbreak, anger, jealousy and loss, another way of capitalising on people's emotions for self-gratification. Ella could hear Mike's voice in her head, telling her that she was always so cynical, so quick to see the negative in everything. It was hard not to.

Ella stopped in front of a tall white plinth that had no one around it.

PAPER CRANE
*I was in the middle of cancer treatment and decided to fold 1000 and
it was while you were helping me fold cranes that you turned to me
and said, 'I'm leaving you.' I stopped folding paper cranes after that.*

The last time Ella had seen paper cranes was on Ling's desk when she had dropped by Mike's office to hand him his lunch, which he'd forgotten to take with him that morning. Leftover lasagne from the night before that looked more like a slew of meat and pastry sheets, the layers merging into a heap in its stained Tupperware container. Although Ella worked from home, she didn't often visit Mike at work, and had noticed that they had changed the office layout since she had been there last.

And that Mike had a new PA.

Mike had been in a meeting, and as Ella handed over the lunch to Ling, her eyes gravitated to the jar of paper cranes sitting on the desk, adding colour to the otherwise muted office palette of corporate greys and lifeless whites.

Ling saw her looking at the jar. 'I make them when I'm having a quiet day. They bring good fortune,' she said, and then smiled sheepishly. 'Or so they say.'

'I've always wanted to learn origami,' Ella said. It had been a blatant lie, but she hadn't known how to respond. She remembered eyeing the framed photo on Ling's desk, angled just enough so that she could see the picture filled with smiling youthful faces. Ling was in the centre of the group, grinning widely, head tipped back, her ebony hair billowing in her face, as if she were drinking in the sky. That image had stuck with Ella – it had been some time since she had been that drunk on life.

Later that night, Mike had come home from work, his mind preoccupied as usual.

'How was the lasagne?' she'd asked.

'I didn't have time to eat it. Work was crazy. I'll eat it tomorrow,' Mike said, not bothering to look up and continuing to scroll through his phone.

'I didn't know you have a new PA,' she pressed.

Mike's head shot up, his eyebrows furrowed. 'Yeah, Ling. She started a couple of months ago,' he said, putting his phone back in his pocket. There was a pause that lasted a second too long. 'I've got work to do,' he said, and walked out of the room.

That had been the end of the conversation, an abrupt full stop to a sentence that hadn't reached its conclusion. Ella had sat with her glass of wine, staring out the window until the room faded out in shadow.

The growing chasm between her and Mike had come in like wisdom teeth, a dull ache they both pretended wasn't there until it became a stabbing pain that couldn't be ignored. The hours Mike spent at work grew longer as the months passed. WON'T BE HOME TILL LATE BIG CASE, he'd text, and Ella would feel relieved. She wouldn't have to play charades that evening. She could remove her mask, even if only for intermission.

Ella shuffled over to the concrete wall behind the plinth.

BRA

I kept buying lacy lingerie to please my now ex-husband. I wanted him to want me. I wanted to be someone else for him. But I was never enough. I realise now that life's too short to be someone you're not.

The black brassiere was attached to the wall, the cups sagging slightly. Ella wondered if this had been deliberate, one last act of defiance against the ex-husband. She resisted the urge to reach out to touch the bra, to feel the lace between her fingers, to smell the lingering drops of sweat that spoke of another truth.

She thought back to the other black bra on that day, when truth and deception had collided in a gamma-ray burst. The confusion, the shock, the dawning realisation; it had all been a blur, the playback in her mind overlaid by a faint nebulous glow. The tangle of limbs, the instinct to cover naked skin, the beads of perspiration like black holes unleashing buried secrets, revealing the extent of the deceit. But what had been most surprising for Ella was the crushing weight of the silence that followed, as if she had entered a vacuum in space.

She felt herself being jostled.

'Sorry,' an older woman said with a smile. She had a row of lines, like sunrays, shooting out from the corners of her eyes.

47

'That's okay,' Ella said automatically.

The woman smiled again and then turned to her companion, taking her hand, a serene picture of unity among the debris of broken hearts.

Ella looked back at the drooping bra on the wall. What could she offer to this Museum of Broken Relationships, she wondered. The mixtape Mike had made for her after she had rejected his initial advances? Give me a chance to make you happy, he'd said. Her wedding ring, now tarnished with broken promises?

No, she knew what she could offer, could see it in her head, on top of its own white wooden plinth: the framed photo of Ling and her friends.

PHOTO
The laughing woman in the centre is the reason why
I'm no longer with my husband.

Ella quickly turned and made her way out of the gallery space, the woman wearing the polka-dotted raincoat shooting her an annoyed look as she hurriedly brushed past her. The swell inside her surged violently, spilling out just as she stepped outside.

She saw the same reel of scenes playing over in her mind in rapid flashes. The paper cranes in the jar. The lacy black bra strung over the side of the bed. The coiled, sweaty limbs. The ebony hair in her hand. Mike's shocked face. Images that would be on permanent display in her own private museum of broken relationships.

At our Grandmother's

Roland Leach

Our teacher gave us the task of writing a poem entitled *At our Grandmother's*. He read out an example and told us to create a distinctive voice. It is always the voice that will make it convincing, he told us - at least twice a day. He means well. The house in the poem sounded a bit creepy as did granny for that matter. Posh though. Lots of references to jewellery, expensive furniture and death.

The problem is I have one surviving grandmother who only drops in two or three times a year. The visit starts out nice and friendly. Granny pulls up in a taxi and treads delicately down the front path with a box of cakes from David Jones, but by late afternoon there's a fight brewing. When Gran gets angry at my Mum she usually pulls out a small silver flask of whisky and lights a cigarette. Two things my Mum does not approve of in her house. The ritual of grandma's exile is then reenacted again, though Mum calls it the *Prodigal Mother Who Doesn't Get a Second Chance.*

I don't even know where my grandmother lives. No one in the family has ever been to her abode so it's difficult to write a poem. My Mum tells me to make it up. Use your imagination, that's what you should be doing in poetry. Teachers have no right getting students to write personal things about family. I try to explain that our teacher wants it to be *authentic.* I say this word in a fancy way knowing it will annoy my Mum. She phffs like a horse, looks me in the eye to see if I am trying to pull a swifty on her and then says in an exaggerated slangy voice, *just make it rhyme, love.*

Mum would have made a good actor, my father often says. That mother of yours can be five women in one day. I'm always hoping one of them will be half decent, he jokes. Mum doesn't smile.

I mention my dilemma to my friend, Laurie, but he fails to show satisfactory sympathy. 'What's your problem? Both my grannies are dead. I'm thinking about writing about the cemetery. My sister says Gothic is in.' I only ever understand half the things Laurie says. As for his sister she is really out there in a strange good-looking sort-of-way. My Mum says she's got it coming. 'What Mum, got what?' 'Do your homework, Robbie. 'But Mummy, my name's not Robbie'. It's a little joke we have.

I try and find out how the rest of the guys are going with their poems and they all seem surprisingly pleased with the assignment. They tell me about their grandparents and how they love them more than their Mum and Dad. They give more expensive presents, things their parents refuse to buy them.

Presents? No one told me about this. The odd sponge cake randomly delivered by an unpredictable ancestor hardly counts.

I scout around and find out about this complex web of relationships between these boys and grandparents. Not one other granny turns up in a taxi with a flask or is thrown out of the house. They are seen regularly, and their place of abode is known and visited, sometimes staying overnight. There is suddenly a totally new world out there I was unaware, that existed like a parallel universe. Sliders or Dr Who style. I seem to be the only one excluded. Laurie doesn't count because of his sister.

I take this information home with a purpose. 'Why have I been deprived of a rich and psychologically rewarding relationship with my grandmother?' I ask. My Mum almost laughs, an act she rarely commits. 'My son, the stand-up. At least you are funnier than your father. That woman you wish to have a rich, psychological relationship, is incapable, at a cognitive and empathetic level, of your desired wish. Most cultures have myths and folklore that explain women like my mother. In Norway they are called the *huldra*. Look it up, kid. Maybe you could write a poem about that'.

And that was as far as I got. Still I knew I was missing out a significant part of my childhood development and definitely missing the story that would explain my mother's relationship with her mother, and explain a lot about Mum. I also start to worry about all the other things that I have failed to notice. I have seen Dennis with his grandparents and he did mention to me how they went on holiday together. Mick has his grandmother living with them. Why have I never registered these families that were different to my own? It was like they were invisible to me.

When dinner is finished I stay seated with my mother. She is reading the newspaper so I sit quietly and stare at her. She doesn't look up but says slowly, 'What are you looking at?'

'My mother,' I say chirpily.

Then she looks up. 'And what have you noticed, my dear son?'

I think quickly. 'Your hair. I always thought it was black, but it is not quite dark enough for black. Is there a name for that colour?

'This is starting to get weird, Rob. Is this about the poem? You're not using me as your grandmother, are you?

'No, you are much too young and attractive.'

'*Now* you are worrying me.'

I think I have her where I want her now. 'I was getting worried about the things I do not notice. I have been at it for a day and there is already a long list'.

'Such as?'

'Given time it might be everything. Well firstly, we are always told we are all equal and that we should be kind and thoughtful to others. Everyone agrees on this: school, you, Dad, the United Nations. But I noticed there are many exceptions'.

'Be specific.'

'Well I can just tell that our teacher doesn't like the new boy from East Pakistan and half the class are nasty and bully him, even though he hasn't done anything wrong.

'So, have you done anything to rectify that state of affairs?'

'No, I told you I just noticed since I have started to think about it. I might have been unpleasant to him as well. Everyone else is.'

'Your point?'

'That's it. There's a whole world that is going unnoticed. I am living in this world but only seeing a tiny angle of it'.

'This is quite profound for a twelve year old. Maybe it's the poetry.'

'On one side of our fence we have Mrs Cann who you do not like because she's a snob and walks around like she can only breathe 'rarefied air,' *your words,* and then Mrs Lamone on the other side who you say is not the *right sort*. The only reason being that she drinks too much coffee, smokes too much and is a divorcee.'

All is quiet. I may have gone too far. Perhaps I should have slowly worked my way up to my mother's flaws.

She has turned away and is looking out the window. I am looking around to see if there is a clear passage if I need to make a dash.

Finally, she says, 'And your father?'

'Dad?' I almost shout out.

'Yes, any astute observations on your father?'

I breathe again.

'Well, you know how you like watching ballet and Dad gets really uncomfortable. He has a name for the guys in the tights. I think it's just because they are wearing tight pants.'

She looks at me and says 'you might be right. About the tight pants that is.'

She folds the newspaper, pulls back her chair and walks out.

I did have some other things to tell her: why are cars built to do over 100 mph when the limit is 65mph and most driving needs to be done at less than 40 mph? The way America invades another country, Vietnam at present, killing thousands and then present themselves convincingly as 'good'? It is 1970 after all! Also, whatever happened to my grandfather. I have never thought about it.

Anyway, I still have a poem to write in less than three days. An *authentic* poem that I have to invent without a grandmother. I went to the library and found a poem by Hart Crane and it's about his grandmother's letters. That's a good idea. I could get little-known gran writing letters to my non-existent grandfather. Hart also calls rain 'soft,' which I like.

After dinner my mother tells me to stay at the table. I am about to ask about grandpa - sounds strange saying it for the first time - but she interjects, 'My turn'.

'Your grandmother was my birthmother but that's all. She left me very early and I was brought up in foster homes. She turned up after I was married. Standing at the flywire door after twenty five years, wanting to come in. She's allowed visits but that's all.'

'What about my grandfather?'

'Took you awhile to ask about him. One of the invisibles, hey? Well there is no grandfather. Unknown, unseen, and unwanted. Anything else?'

I nod and she gets up to leave but I ask if she has any letters written by Gran.

'No, just a postcard' she says, 'It was sent from Aden in the early days. Despite all I have said about her she was an adventurous woman. Great shot of the camels. I'll get it for you but I want it back – for the camel not my mother'.

I finished up inventing a scene where she is writing home to her daughter from a tent she was living in, outside of Aden. It was not exactly 'at my grandmother's' but I wrote a short note telling my teacher that my grandmother was a bohemian, who travelled the world and had many abodes. He wrote a note back telling me not to use 'abode' so often. Nevertheless, he was impressed with my poem, probably because after constantly reminding us to be specific I described her 'living quarters' as a 'black goat-hair tent' and gave the Arabic name of bayt al-shar. I got 88%.

Three months later a policeman came to the door and asked for Mum. Her mother had been found dead in her house. She was asked to go with him.

We all went there a few days later to pick up her personal items. There wasn't much and as I looked around her home thought that I would have liked to have asked my grandmother about the desert, camels, and Aden.

I knew I would have written a better poem had I seen the one room flat, with one plate, a cup & saucer, one pot and a small heater.

The Emerald Leaf

Judith A Wallis

In the aisle of his tiny church on Bullock Street, Father Malloy stood polishing his bi-focals with a large handkerchief. A slight tremor in his hands caused him to fumble. The spectacles finally in place, he peered up at the image of Christ in the garden pictured in the stained-glass window. Was that a hole? Had a piece somehow fallen out? Uncertain, he removed his shoes, climbed onto a pew and stretching up, gripped the sill. A closer examination revealed there was indeed a hole. An emerald leaf was missing — part of the foliage that surrounded the feet of the Christ.

Malloy returned his stockinged feet to the floor, made a thorough but unsuccessful search of the area beneath the window then pulling on his shoes, hurried out into the street. Again he searched, his only reward a wad of gum stuck to the sole of his shoe. His aged fingers sought the comfort of his rosary. The missing glass would have to be replaced. What would it cost? There was no money. The provision of food and shelter for families forced from their smallholdings by the drought had drained all resources. Ignoring the dust coating the hem of his cassock, Father Malloy returned to the church and with a mosaic of rainbows reflected from the stained glass dancing over his snow-white hair, bowed his head in prayer.

Parked beside the empty water trough in front of the general store, Liam Morgan sat motionless in the cab of his dilapidated farm truck. Beside him, young Emily, her nose level with the dashboard, stared ahead. On the drive into town Liam had explained to his daughter his need to cull their dying stock for the second time in a year.

Liam sighed. His own childhood home had nestled amid hills and mountains whose grand height claimed a generous portion of the firmament; a place of abundant rain. Here, the land ran flat forever. The brazen blue dipped on all sides, boxing them in, prisoners to the sun's relentless heat. Liam removed his hat and wiped his brow. His body smelt of sweat and he wondered what it would be like to take a real bath.

'Can I go to Mrs Casey's?'

At the sound of Emily's voice he turned and seeing afresh her small pinched face and sad eyes, his heart seemed to falter in his chest. 'Yes, love, that's a good idea. I'll come by and pick you up in an hour.'

Emily ran barefoot along the grass strip at the edge of the road. Only now there was no grass, just hard clay and the occasional ragged clump of weed. As she turned the corner by the church a sudden pain halted her progress and she sat down to inspect the sole of her foot. Blood welled along a cut. She licked a finger and wiped. More blood appeared. A thin trickle ran down her foot.

Beside her something glittered amongst the stones and Emily picked it up. Shaped like a leaf and with bubbles at one end, the emerald-green glass shone in the sun. Holding it to her eye, she squinted through it. The effect was magical. The street and all in it was awash with green. Lush, cool green and the little bubbles looked like raindrops.

Still holding the glass leaf to her eye Emily limped her way to Mrs Casey's front gate. Not so long ago, Mrs Casey's small home had been screened by luxuriant foliage and colourful flowers. But as season followed season, each as dry as the last, the plants had died, disclosing an ugly, grey fibro shack. All that remained of Mrs Casey's much-loved garden was a single eucalypt and the lifeless swing that hung from a bough.

With the help of her glass leaf and a lively imagination, Emily restored the cool shadowy pathways of the original garden and eager to share the wonderful green world she had discovered, quickened her pace and leapt the two concrete steps to the front porch. A large ginger cat, startled by Emily's sudden arrival, bolted for safety. He shot past Emily's legs causing her to shriek, hop sideways and fall.

'Emily dear, can you hear me? Emily? Oh, love.' Mrs Casey's blue veined hands swept the hair from Emily's face and tapped her pale cheeks before rubbing her small icy hands. But Emily did not stir. Little by little and with much puffing, Mrs Casey managed to pull her indoors out of the sun. Then taking Emily's hands within her own, waited for her eyes to open. Moments later Emily woke and rubbed the back of her head.

'Oh, I have a lump.' She sat up and smiled at her rescuer.

'Thank goodness you are all right. Are your parents in town?'

'Just Dad and me. I'm not hurt, truly.'

'Just the same, let me look at your head. As you say, a lump. Now your foot, please.' Emily raised a grubby foot. 'Hmmm. A wash and a sticking plaster will fix that. Then I'll make us a nice cup of tea.'

When the teacups were empty, Emily pulled the glass leaf from her pocket. 'Look, Mrs Casey. Look through this,' she said.

Her eye to the glass, Mrs Casey stared about the room. She moved to the doorway and gazed out over the straggly scrub that edged the dry riverbed across the road. The green colour stirred memories. Shapes, stiff and brittle, softened beneath her gaze as deep within, her sense of loss eased and hope crept in. She placed a hand over her heart.

'It's quite magical. I really do feel cool, refreshed. Thank you, dear,' she said and drew Emily into a hug as Liam Morgan appeared at the door.

'Daddy!' Emily ran to greet her father. Mrs Casey followed and after a brief account of Emily's fainting spell, stood waving goodbye until the truck turned the church corner. On her way back to the house she lingered on the path. In her mind's eye she saw a flourishing garden: green of every hue, dark moss, olive and the bright yellow-green of new growth, all springing up, full of life. She heard the patter of rain on the roof; saw the river running smooth as silk and the white herons fishing.

Back indoors she took from the back of a cupboard old seed catalogues and gardening magazines. And as she turned the pages reading Latin names and imagining where and how the planting should be done, Mrs Casey found herself daring to hope, hope that swelled and became a possibility.

All the way home Emily gazed through her glass leaf, seeing the countryside green and beautiful. When they reached the farm she passed the leaf to her father and to please her, he held it to his eye and looked out across the desolate landscape. The rush of wonder took him by surprise and he turned a full circle. Beneath his gaze grass grew, sheep fattened and he felt his shoulders relax. God willing, he thought, the farm could look this way again. Yes. It could happen. He held out his hand and in a voice gruff with emotion said, 'Come along, Emily. Let's see what your mother has prepared for tea.'

Later in the evening, when Emily complained of a headache and stumbled on her way to bed, her concerned parents phoned the doctor for advice.

'You say she fell, hit her head?'

'Yes.'

'A mild concussion is most likely. I would like to be sure though. Can you bring her into the cottage hospital? I have a birth to attend but expect to be back in town soon after midnight.'

For Emily's parents, the drive into town was slow. Liam did his best, driving carefully to avoid the ruts and potholes of the country road while Emily dozed in her mother's arms, the green glass leaf, wrapped in Liam's handkerchief, clutched in her hand.

At the hospital Emily climbed willingly into the big white bed. She slid the glass leaf beneath her pillow and closing her eyes, appeared to sleep. Several times during the night she woke with a jerk. She muttered about rain, about swimming in the creek and once, sat bolt upright, declaring she could smell the roses in Mrs Casey's garden.

The Doctor arrived at daybreak. While confident Emily was in no danger, he suggested she and her mother stay at the hospital another 24 hours. 'I came through fairly heavy rain on the way back. With luck, we will get some too,' he added.

Emily pulled the glass leaf from beneath the pillow. 'Look. This is my magic leaf. It makes everything green again.'

Laughing, the doctor patted Emily's hand. 'Keep your fingers crossed,' he called as he left the ward.

Liam Morgan returned to his farm exhausted after the long night. There had been forecasts of rain for a month but none this far south. His boots dragged as he carried cans of gasoline out to the truck.

He drove across the dry paddocks, his rifle and ammunition on the seat beside him, his unseeing eyes fixed on the horizon, his mind grappling with the task ahead.

Thirty minutes later, something in the landscape seemed to change and he rubbed a weary hand across his eyes. Curious, he looked again.

'Clouds!' The word erupted in a great yell from his throat. The doc. was right. It was going to rain. Liam's raucous laughter startled a flock of crows. They took to the air flying high into the fast darkening sky.

Still laughing, Liam spun the wheel carving a wide arc in the dust as he turned the ute for home. On the way he thought of Emily's strange leaf-shaped piece of glass and how, when he looked through it, he had seen fields of fresh green grass. Emily thought it was magic. Perhaps it was.

Emily lay asleep in the cottage hospital, the glass leaf on the bedside table. Outside rain streaked the windows and gurgled down pipes. It fell harder. Fell faster. Filled creeks and dams and spat through the hole in the stained glass window of the church on Bullock Street corner.

Late the next morning, when the pub had run dry and the back slapping and cheering was over, Emily returned home from the hospital bright and happy.

The following Sunday the little church filled to overflowing as packed like sardines in the pews, their wet weather gear left steaming in the vestibule, the farming community gathered to give thanks.

Emily sat with her parents and Mrs Casey and as the offering bowl passed from hand to hand, she drew from her purse the glass leaf and solemnly placed it with the coins in the plate. Liam understood and smiling with his eyes, directed her attention to the altar, where instead of the usual arrangement of artificial flowers, someone had placed a crystal glass of green grass.

Corvus Orru

Wendy Langridge

This is the man who is making a road, a double highway. A civil engineer: he wears a hi-vis vest and Blundstone boots with steel caps. The yellow hardhat he invariably forgets on the passenger seat of the ute. In the mornings he pushes his keepcup of coffee into the drink holder, and drives the short distance from his house the size of a letterbox to arrive on site at dawn.

Roads are made of bitumen mostly, composed of the by-products of crude oil. Bitumen is churned out of a machine, rather like toothpaste from a tube, and then a steam roller goes back and forth and flattens it. Nothing to the process, really. That's what most people think; nothing to it. If only they knew. The engineer thinks of roads all the time. Roads lead to, and away from, places. They connect farms, outposts and villages, towns, cities and countries. They are the veins of civilisation. Some roads are mere tracks in the sand. Some are great throbbing monstrosities. Some, again, are metaphorical. The road to the civil engineer's heart is a bumpy, pot-holed one. On site, in the solitude, thoughts of roads are sometimes the only things that go through his head. Occasionally the one he'll think of is Roscoe, where he lives in Sydney. Roscoe Street slopes gently upwards, from the sea, and from the beach, where the light splinters the sky. Early in the morning it's quiet enough that he lopes up it without having to watch for cars. The barista might be opening up the coffee shop, putting out the A-board, and he'll nod his head in greeting. Other times the engineer won't think of roads at all but watch the low dip of the sky, as though he must duck to walk under a hammock. Occasionally he'll get an image of a bed, of white sheets and a suntanned arm flung across them, and sometimes he might glimpse a face, the blue of eyes, stubble on the chin, but he tries not to think of these things. These reminders do not belong here, with the road, and the job.

He checks the work that was done yesterday, pausing to stoop and touch the gritty surface, and he walks alongside the work that's to be done today. He tilts his head, closes one eye, and runs his gaze along the lines and horizontals, checking for flaws. Then he turns the other way and looks into the distance where the highway is headed, through the hills and across the scrubby landscape. This morning he's distracted by a crow hopping in the scree, on one leg. Does the poor bugger only have the one?

By the time he returns to his ute his phone is ringing in the cabin. And he's no longer alone. Doors are slamming, men are whistling, calling to one another, bantering. Amanda and Evie, who man the flags, are waiting to complain to him about the heat to come. The temperature's already sitting on twenty-five degrees, they tell him. Sorry girls, he says, we've got a way to go before you can down tools. Ugh, they groan.

Dingo has rescued his phone. Dingo's just a kid, all of eighteen, but he's quick. Nicknamed for the colour of his hair, white, his propensity to please, and his occasional dogged waywardness, he's holding the phone out to the engineer. You're meant to take the fucking thing with you, the boss says in the engineer's ear. His boss thinks he's a little odd, a tad solitary, but the man keeps giving him more responsibility, more leeway, so he must be doing something right. There's a problem looming, something to do with the town ahead of them and a horse race, but his boss says he'll sort it. He's just giving him a heads-up. Wouldn't do any harm to go down the pub Friday and put in an appearance, orright, mate? Right, the engineer says. Dingo pulls the ute door open, indicates the engineer should get in. Gotta go down to Joe, he says. Problem with D9.

At lunch the engineer sits on the shaded step of the pre-fab, his boots in the dirt, and scoffs his cold stir fry of beef and noodles out of the plastic container. A floret of broccolini drops to the earth and he remembers the one-footed crow. He wonders where he is, and whether he should keep something back for him. He sips at his sparkling water. *Sparkling?* What are you, some kind of poof? Dingo had said with a cheeky grin when the engineer first arrived. Yeah, mate. Absolutely, he'd replied, cracking a smile and smoothing over any awkwardness. That's probably the sum total of any social conversation he's had with the kid. Sometimes, although he's only in his early forties, he feels like an old man alongside the boy.

He doesn't know why, but he thinks Dingo knows. How, he isn't sure.

The engineer lives with Liam in Bondi, in an apartment two roads up from the beach. They have a black and white cat called Coco that keeps Liam company during the weeks the engineer is away. Liam is a librarian and when the engineer is home they rise at the same time in the morning and they'll walk together up Roscoe Street to the tram stop and to Liam's work. The engineer will have the first coffee of the day with him, and then he'll walk back to Bondi. Sometimes, if he's missing Liam, he'll go to the library at noon and sit quietly and read, pausing every now and again to watch his friend at work, waiting until Liam looks up and finds him there. It will be enough and he will return to the apartment and Coco. Sometimes, when no-one's looking, Liam blows him a goodbye kiss, which turns him inside out.

Late Friday and the engineer is packing up when he hears it. A crow. It's been a blistering day, his neck is grimy with sweat, but he slots the dusty spirit level into its place above the toolbox and turns from the back of the ute. The crow's wobbling on the fence line, on his one leg, silhouetted against the sun, making a series of slow clicks and awks. The engineer glances around but everyone has cleared off—he's always the last to go. There's an apple core on the dashboard, a remnant from brekky, and he retrieves it and holds it out. The crow turns its head, balefully glares one eye at him then flaps, lifts itself heavily from the wire and floats in, its black beak like an arrowhead, its feathers billowing like a cape. It snatches the core from his fingers and is gone.

The town's pub is a sprawling old Queenslander with ceiling fans and sepia-coloured photographs of sombre Victorians pegged to the wooden panelling. Dingo's kept the engineer a place up at the bar, at the end where he prefers to be, and five of them sit in a row and try to act inconspicuous, hard when they're all in hi-vis vests. Some of the crew bring their families and place them in the closest rentals they can find and Friday nights they go home to their wives and girlfriends. The guys at the bar are either single, Dingo for instance, or their wives and girlfriends objected to being moved. Amanda and Evie are locals. What's left of the crew spend the weekend at the camp close to the construction site. The engineer keeps to himself. He does his laundry. He reads. He writes emails to his sister on his laptop, letters to Liam on real paper with a real pen. He finds it easier to write to Liam than to talk to him on the phone. Tomorrow he will tell him about the crow. Perhaps Liam will give it a name. What's a good name for a crow? *Corvus orru*, he remembers, is its scientific name. The word *Torresian* comes into it too, somewhere. Corey, then?

He brings himself back to the present with a gulp of beer. The condensation runs down the side of the glass and soaks into the coaster, a coaster depicting a man in a business shirt sitting at a laminated kitchen table while a smiling wife carries his dinner towards him. He thinks about Liam and wonders if he's cooking Friday night salmon, and humming at the same time, and whether Coco is waiting for a morsel of crispy skin. Only two more weeks until he goes home. He can cross off another day tonight. Gossip about Amanda and Evie reaches the engineer, but he's listening with only half an ear. He's thinking about how he can open the conversation with the barman about closing the road to the town.

He downs his beer and rises to go to the toilet, but before he does so he leans across and puts in a last order, and as he leaves he recognises a man coming up the stairs.

He's washing his hands when the door opens. Looking up, he sees the man in the mirror, the man he recognised. He's seen him before, in Sydney, and knows why he's followed him into the washroom. Old history. Pre-Liam. The man sidles up behind, the engineer braces himself. But the door opens again and Dingo enters—they exchange a glance—while the man casually sidesteps and reaches for the soap dispenser. The engineer dries his hands, listens to the steady stream of the boy's urine hitting metal. Then he leans against the doorjamb and says something to him about the work. He's not sure what he's saying, he just knows he won't abandon Dingo. The man finishes up and with one glance—a glance that says it all, you got away this time—exits the washroom. Dingo shakes himself. The engineer gazes absently at a scrunched up paper towel discarded on the tiles. The kid goes over to the basin. There's the soothing sound of running water.

Monday, Corey the crow is waiting, lurching on the fence line in the dawn light. The engineer holds out a rasher of bacon, furled like a ribbon, and the bird flaps and lifts itself from the wire. He places the bacon in the palm of his hand and the crow lands awkwardly, putting out its one foot and curving its talons around his finger. Prickly but solid. Corey teeters, stretches his sharp beak forward, secures the bacon. He stares at the engineer, then lifts his black obsidian body, raises himself into the air, and the engineer watches until the crow is a charcoal dot in the chalky sky.

Sweet! Dingo calls, ambling onto site. He must've walked from the camp.

The engineer wipes his bacony hand on the back of his strides. You're up early.

The kid shrugs. Couldn't sleep. He holds out a flask. Coffee? I brought extra.

Ta, the engineer says, and holds out his keepcup. Dingo pours. They avoid each other's eyes.

Know anything about crows? the kid says.

Greta

Craig Billingham

In the second week of November I finished university and moved back to my parents' place so I could live rent-free. The intention, which was more like an oath I'd sworn to myself, was to depart for London early in the New Year. Daniel, as younger brothers do, had taken over my bedroom, which meant I got the smaller room at the front of the house. Greta's bedroom was out of bounds.

My new room contained a desk and an ironing board, an exercise bike, a vacuum cleaner, and a single bed. There was also a large bookcase, which was a touch embarrassing – I'd studied English and Philosophy but I hadn't excelled at either. I pushed my boxes under the bed and left the backpack below the window.

On the first evening it was humid. We ate a meal together. The ceiling fan wobbled above our heads, as it had for as long as I could remember. My father opened a bottle of wine. Daniel and I drank beer.

'I'm glad you're home,' my mother said, touching my forearm as she did so.

I knew she was thinking of Greta, my sister, her youngest child. Greta had left home some six months earlier, and since then our conversations, regardless of their content, were cut to the shape of her absence.

The idiocy of planning to arrive in London in the middle of January was lost on no one but me.

'You'll freeze your balls off,' my father warned, or something along those lines.

I promised myself I would not complain about the cold, about the hours pinched from daylight, at least not to him. I'd be single-minded, optimistic. I'd learn that life away from home requires an editorial frame of mind. Cross out the negatives. Make notations in the margins. Get on with things.

Bored one day, somewhere in the no man's land of early December, I set the stepladder beneath the manhole and fetched down from the roof cavity a box of old belongings, school reports, mixed tapes, that type of thing. In one of her notebooks Greta had transcribed the following quotation: *In Russia peat fires can burn underground for weeks on end. They are tended by fire fighters, controlled but not extinguished, awaiting heavy rain.* That's her, I thought: a self-portrait in fewer than thirty words.

Greta telephoned on December 18th, for our father's birthday. Would she come home for Christmas? She would not, because Christmas was gross and racist and immoral.

'She used the word 'fascist,'' my father reported, his large head tilted on his neck and shoulders. 'How could she use that word?'

My parents clung to the idea that Greta was going through a phase, as though each outburst was a rite of passage, but that was the wrong way to characterise my sister. The squat she was living in, and I knew it even then, was a station of the cross.

Christmas Day was hot, the festive spirit forced. For lunch my father stuffed a pink snapper, wrapped it in foil and baked it gently on the barbecue. There was a magnum of champagne and there was a kilo of cooked prawns. There was beer and wine. There were crackers and party hats.

'You look like such a dick,' my brother said.

'To Greta,' proposed my mother, and everyone raised their glass, though typically my sister's name was a brake on bonhomie.

After lunch I went out to the pool, where, floating on the back of an inflatable red dragon, I ate a second helping of plum pudding and brandy sauce. I'd like to think I thought of Greta, but it's just as likely I did my best to think of anything but her. It wasn't the first time she'd taken off – it was the third – but it was the longest period without a member of the family having seen her.

I dozed off, dumbly adrift, and I must have slept until my father woke me. He was on the edge of the pool, still wearing his party hat, calling my name and prodding me with the pool cleaner. He hadn't bothered to empty out the basket.

'Jesus Christ,' he said. 'I almost dived in.'

I laughed at that, at the thought of it, and he laughed too – we couldn't help it. It had been years since my father had last been in the pool. Not old but ageing rapidly. A pastry cutter might have found his former self, buried within the dough.

The first time Greta ran away she was nine and I was twelve. My mother called the police. She spoke hurriedly, with sharp intakes of breath.

'No,' she said, 'not since lunch. I think so. Yes. The boys are at home.

Yes, with my husband. Please, please. Thankyou.'

The Sergeant on duty said to wait, to calm down, that young children mostly came home of their own accord, or else were found wandering nearby. The local patrol cars would be alerted.

'Try not to panic,' my mother said. 'That's what he suggested: try not to panic. That was his advice. This sort of thing happens all the time.'

'Right,' was my father's response to that. 'Ride around between here and the school, but I want you home every ten minutes. Understand? Here – take my watch.'

I did as I was told, and on my fifth pit stop Greta was in the lounge room.

'She was with the neighbours' dog,' my father said. 'Just lying there, in the backyard. The dog hadn't barked all afternoon, which everyone thought was strange.'

I spent New Year's Eve in The Rocks with some friends from uni. We met at eight. At eleven thirty we walked to Observatory Hill to watch the fireworks. The best spots were taken, covered with blankets and hampers, and all around were faces flushed from alcohol or sunburn.

Eventually someone started a countdown. Champagne corks popped. Couples paired off and kissed as fireworks exploded above the harbour. People of all ages linked arms, sang *Auld Lang Syne* and danced. The Bridge proffered a smiley face, like a benevolent dictator. Be happy, be happy, be happy, the annual injunction.

I kissed a girl I knew only vaguely – she'd arrived with a classmate from *Twentieth Century American Literature*, but he didn't seem to mind – and then I left without saying goodbye. I walked towards Wynyard Station. The military precision of the firework display had depressed me, in the same way that adults wearing bicycle helmets always depresses me. Is there anything more infantile than organised fun? Anything more prescriptive? From Town Hall I caught the night bus home.

The second time Greta ran away she was fourteen. By then I'd been living in Newtown for a year, but I caught the train back to my parents' place immediately. My mother had called the police again, and again they'd told her not to panic. She and my father waited up all night. I went to bed late, but I did not sleep.

A police car brought Greta home at 9am the following morning. She and a friend had hidden in the public toilet at *Westfield*, waiting for it to close. When everyone had gone home, they'd come out of hiding and smeared boot polish and peanut butter over three shop windows, the butcher's most thoroughly – one of the officers said it looked like pebbledash. Although not part of their plan, Greta and her accomplice had been locked in overnight.

Asked why she'd done it, Greta replied, 'Because everything's so disgusting, and no one cares.'

Greta was arrested on Australia Day, which we found out because the mother of Daniel's girlfriend saw her on *National Nine News*. There'd been a land rights march in the city, culminating in a rally at Hyde Park. From the footage I saw, on the *ABC*, it looked as though the police were heavy handed, using shields and horses. My sister was one of seven to chain themselves to a tree – the Fig Tree Seven, the press called them, but also ratbags and sponges, and a commentator from *The Australian* used the term 'ne'er-do-wells,' which sent my father apoplectic.

'Who the hell does he think we are?' he said. 'Where the hell does he think we live?'

Greta was charged with affray and causing a public nuisance. She was released the following day, into the custody of my parents.

My father wasn't the kind of man to jump at an opportunity to use a leaf-blower, but that's what he was doing as I watched him from the lounge room window – blowing leaves down the driveway, out on to street. He walked slowly, relieved to be alone, away for a short while from the theatre of his family. Every now and then he kicked at the blue extension cord, untangling it from beneath his feet. It had been four days since Greta had come home, and two days since she'd left.

'I hate this house,' she'd screamed. 'I hate everything about it.'

I turned twenty-one on February 8th, which was the day I confirmed my flight. After lunch, my mother and I washed the dishes.

'You don't have to,' she said. 'Not today.'

But I didn't mind, in fact I was glad to do it. I know how boring that must sound, but after Greta's two days at home, boring didn't seem so awful.

'If I'm being honest,' my mother said, 'I don't want you to go to Europe. Is that selfish?'

Everything she held good and dear had been acutely spurned by Greta, and now her eldest son was leaving.

'I'll be back,' I said, and my mother did her best to laugh.

Perhaps Greta was right to act on her disgust instead of carping from the sofa. Perhaps Greta was strong and the rest of us were weak.

For leaving drinks I met six friends in Newtown. We played pool in the
back room and drank jugs of beer. After two hours Leonard and Omid and
Kathy and I went for dinner. I was seated next to Leonard, who at that time
was in a relationship with Omid. Kathy's new boyfriend, a Psych nurse, was
on night shift at the *Royal Prince Alfred* hospital.

'Do you have a place to live?' asked Omid.

'With a mate from uni,' I said.

'Everyone lives with Andy,' said Leonard, 'when they first arrive.'

Omid had family in London — she had family everywhere, except
in Tehran, where she was born — and she was the only one at the table
with firsthand knowledge of Europe. She and Leonard planned to travel in
June, though as it turned out they broke up in May.

On leaving the restaurant Kathy and I walked together to the station.
It had rained heavily while we were inside, but already the footpath and
the road were dry.

'And your sister?' she asked. 'What's happening with her?'

'She'll be fine,' I said, but I knew it was a lie.

I came home five months later, for the start of Greta's trial. She and three
others had been accused of smashing windows at *David Jones*, entering the
store, and setting piles of expensive clothes on fire. The damage bill was in
the tens of thousands. She pleaded guilty.

'You seem very angry,' the prosecutor said.

'Of course,' said Greta. 'As everyone should be.'

My parents and I stared at the floor. Daniel was off somewhere,
doing something with his girlfriend. It was the last of Greta's trials that I
attended. I do not visit her in jail, but I try to see her when she's out

Jesus Sticker

Phil Enchelmaier

We gave Mitch a shit-tonne about the Jesus sticker on the Mazda 2 he'd saved up all summer for, but by April he still hadn't taken it off. He was stubborn and hated doing anything if he felt like someone else had decided for him. We weren't dickheads, we didn't make a thing of it – general good-natured piss-taking aside, like, we started calling him the Priest and if his door was closed we'd make paedophilia/choirboy jokes, which led to his door being closed more often, giving us more opportunity for said general good-natured piss-taking. It was Rhys, the new Arts-Law double major, who went and made it a thing.

If it's supposed to be a joke, I don't find it funny, he said.

Mitch said nothing. Just stared at a landslide in Burma, which led into a promo for *The Bachelor*. Always the peacemaker among housemates, I explained to Arts-Law that Mitch had bought the car from a religious redhead who parked up the street. He told her he'd seen the sticker on her car and she asked which sticker – the one with "JESUS SAVES" inside a fish, and should she get out the holy water? Or the one listing make, model and price? They laughed together, *Hahaha…* I saw the whole thing.

Do you want to fuck her? asked Johnno, to which Mitch replied I have a girlfriend. That wasn't a *no*, because even though he was loyal to Chloe, we all knew he didn't like her. She hung out for two hours every Friday night, only Friday night – always the same routine, she'd come over and cook satay chicken with pasta and he would have bought a cake or a tub of icecream and they'd eat it all in front of us as if we weren't even there, then they'd go up to his room which he would have spent the day cleaning, then half an hour later she'd get dressed and go home and he'd come downstairs and he and I'd drink beer on the back deck in silence, which he craved…

The ads were done and the hot weathergirl was on now. Rhys was the only one whose eyes weren't glued to the screen. I wasn't sure if he was gay or just one of those male feminists, I mean we were all totally respectful of women and speaking for myself I never fantasized about Weathergirl in a denigrating or disempowering manner – more often than not she was on top, and I always sought consent, and she always said yes. But Rhys planted himself between us and the TV and asked how does it look having a car with a rainbow flag sticker parked next to a car with a Jesus sticker? Zak the pothead ventured a who-gives-a-fuck-it's-just-a-sticker. Rhys said it's more than a sticker, it's a symbol of oppression (quoting Dawkins, chapter and verse) – of women, of the homosexuals, of indigenous peoples, and what about all the kids those priests molested? That prompted said good-natured piss-taking paedophilia jokes, and *that* fired up Johnno on a rant about the evils of organized religion – of organized *anything* – because he'd just learned his one-act play had been rejected by the Student Theatre Guild. The conversation petered out after that. I reassured them privately that Mitch would take the sticker off, he just needed time, needed to feel like it was his decision, like he wasn't being pressured.

The next day Mitch pulled in with another bumper sticker. "REAL MEN LOVE GOD". Above and slightly to the right of "JESUS SAVES". That night: another house meeting. Mitch is stubborn, I remind my housemates he doubles down when threatened. But there's Rhys marching out of Sema again, and Johnno fuming about the distortion of Christ's teachings (kindly tutor having suggested edits to improve one-act), and Zak the pothead flinging the neighbour's cat back over the fence into their swimming pool because he hates anything that ruins the vibe. Mitch wasn't there; he'd gone out with Chloe. Her parents forked out for a five-star hotel buffet dinner each time they were in town, once every three months, and it was this, solely, that Mitch was staying in the relationship for. But when he pulled back into the drive that night I could tell it hadn't gone well so I got a few beers from the fridge and we sat on the deck. After a half hour he muttered that Chloe had broken up with him. Why, I asked. Because of the stickers. Said she couldn't be with someone religious, since she was a student of science, and the one thing they had in common, the basis of their future together – fifty-year marriage, grandchildren and camper vans and battered cod and cool wet grains of sand between their toes – was their belief in a rational, godless universe. And he was throwing it away! He reckoned she must have been looking for a way out because she just dropped the bomb and scurried off. I said okay then did you tell her the stickers are just a joke to piss off your P.C. housemates? He drained a warmish eighth of his lager and said no, the stickers aren't about pissing anyone off.

So I asked him point blank if he was, after all, religious. He shook his head. Still an atheist. Maybe an agnostic. I said that's a slippery slope. I mean I'm agnostic, I told him, but in the right circumstances (T-boning Weathergirl at the lights, both of us miraculously surviving yet permanently crippled, bonded in our pain but not too much pain, her having miracle healing leading to conversion, insisting I experience same or else), I could see myself cracking.

And so I asked again if it was about scoring with the religious redhead who sold him the car/some other religious hottie as yet unknown to us/some religious dude and were they both, coincidentally, exploring their sexuality?

No, no, no.

And then he went to bed. I think I heard him sobbing into his pillow. Or wanking. Probably both.

Within a week he'd added "GOD ROCKS". Within a month: "FEAR GOD" "WWJD" and "HONK IF YOU LOVE JESUS, TEXT IF YOU WANT TO MEET HIM." The battle raged on: speeches, denunciations, ultimatums – all met with his silence. He didn't say a word when we handed him the eviction notice. Typed out and co-signed by all the housemates, me included. I scribbled my name next to the others – it was the only thing I could have done; I'm a peacemaker. Still, the sight of his stickered car rolling away down the street filled me with a regret I hadn't felt since when I was a kid and I'd accidentally kick the plug out of my bubble bath and couldn't find it to put it back in before all the water drained out.

The house fell apart after that. Johnno moved to the theatre district of London and wound up a happily married plumber in Sussex. Good for him. Still left us in the lurch, rent-wise, until we got Stacey in, but then that ended up being a whole thing. In my defence, I thought I was alone in the house. And it's not like there was a lock on her bedroom door, it wasn't even closed all the way, so I went in, saw her chest of drawers, the bed, pile of laundry on it, lovely and folded and fresh, jeans on bottom, smalls on top... Anyway that night I had to crash at Mitch's place. He didn't ask what happened; we sat on his balcony and drank beers in silence, and I thought, what a good friend.

I didn't last long in my next place either. I tried to argue that since her particular item of clothing had already fallen off the Hills Hoist it would need to go through the wash again anyway, and therefore what's the difference? That didn't fly, so back I was drinking beers with Mitch. His new housemates were cool with the stickers apparently, even after he added four more, but it got some passer-by in the mood to spray the anarchist symbol on their front door and the landlord was pissed and it was them or him, and so it was him with me again... and round it went like that. The more places I got booted from the more I understood how it felt for Mitch. The abuse, the agony of fresh-hurled eggs dripping from "JESUS LOVES YOU". How much it's possible for humans to hate other humans. Even when you haven't done anything wrong – my legal aid

caseworker told me it wasn't illegal, necessarily, I'm sure I heard right.
Man, she was sweet. Forty-something, frizzy hair, but had a smile that
made me feel like it was Christmas…

Anyway I didn't want to talk about it then, not after she was reassigned, and
I don't now. I don't need a caseworker, or a psychotherapist, or a former
lecturer who bones his students assuring me I'm not so bad after all. None
of them can help. None of them can save me. What I need is a Mitch. A
friend who's there for me no matter what. A friend who doesn't ask, doesn't
tell, just takes me as I am and me him.
     But Mitch left; he got in that car and drove away. I'd come to his latest
digs in need of shelter, like so many times before, only to see his car rolling
down the street just that instant. Gaze stubbornly set on the road ahead, a
road he knew he must travel, alone, while former housemates stood at the
gate wishing him and his stickers far away.
     I didn't wish him away, I wished him back. But he didn't answer my
calls, didn't text, didn't honk, didn't descend from heaven, didn't incarnate
into my desperate life. I locked and looked for him, for his Mazda 2, as
days and months amounted to decades.

The funniest thing – what makes me laugh whenever I think of it, which is
often, and I get some weird looks from passers-by – the funniest thing is
I haven't seen a single Jesus sticker since. In my fifteen minutes' browsing
time on Terminal 3 at the library yesterday I searched "Jesus Stickers' and
couldn't find a single one. Maybe I misspelt. But I like to think he bought
them all. I like to think he got rich somehow, contacted every manufacturer
of Jesus stickers the world over and bought out all their stock for all time.
That car must be completely unroadworthy by now. Every inch covered a
thousand times over with the words that cause so many people so much
pain. All those words of faith and love and sacrifice, so sure, so certain
the rest of us just can't bear it. Maybe that was his plan all along – to take
the Jesus stickers of the world on himself, and suffer in our place, that we
might have peace.

Man Versus Fish

M.J. Reidy

Kaz had a dream. Two, if you counted her fantasy of appearing on *A Current Affair*– not as a petty crim ripping someone off, more as a reluctant heroine, or a rags-to-riches star like Kardashian, with the ass to boot. The other dream was simple, but far more elusive, a bit like trying to come down off the gear. Dwayne – eight times she'd broken up with him, and eight times they'd gotten back together. Now, on their ninth stretch, they were somehow engaged. But by Friday, she'd get rid of him. For real this time.

In readiness for the breakup, Kaz began to chuck out things he'd given her over the years. A faulty rice cooker. A TV that only picked up the ABC kid's channel. A book he'd given her for her birthday, *'Why does he fall asleep after sex?,'* leopard skin G-strings, now stretched as thin as dental floss.

Her mobile vibrated in her pocket, making her jump.

Dwayne. 'Yep.'

'Hey,' he said. She could see him, toying with the flavour saver on his lip that was fifteen years out of date. 'Had a big win today. Lady Luna got up.'

'I had a win too,' she said, considering the pile, the bra cups pointing at the ceiling as if in tribute to Madonna's *Vogue*.

She could hear the crackle as he inhaled a cigarette. 'I'll take ya out for dinner. Had a hundred bucks on the filly's nose. My shout.'

'Alright,' she said. She stared at her wardrobe, wondering which would be the best break-up outfit. Nothing too happy or bright. Maybe something low cut, showing off a bit of skin. Enough so he'd feel sorry for himself when she delivered the news.

'Love ya,' he said.

'Yep.' She wiggled the engagement ring from her finger.

'To the fuckin' moon, Kaz. Don't ever forget it.'

As they waited for their spring rolls, Dwayne tried his best to entertain her, shoving two of the chopsticks up his gums, doing his Bug's Bunny-Ching-Chong-China-man impression. The old Kaz would have laughed, but she remained tight-lipped. Composed. Yep, she thought, this was the new Kaz, about to rise out of the flames like an ass-kicking phoenix.

She rehearsed her break-up spiel, chanting it under her breath. Last time she'd told him her mother was dying, the Big C: 'Can't look after Mum *and* you,' she'd said, faking tears, putting on a real Hollywood performance. But he'd called her Mum the next day, punching a hole in Kaz's kitchen wall when he found out.

Kaz tried not to think about it. She leant back in her seat, gazing at a fish tank behind Dwayne. It was lit with a greenish-blue light, casting an eerie glow across Dwayne's face. The tank was small, containing only one fish. The fish was long and sinewy, sleek. She watched as the lone fish swam back and forth up the tank, watching her intently.

'What's up?' Dwayne said.

She stood up, swapping seats so she sat side-on to the tank. 'That fish. It's creeping me out.'

Dwayne turned around and stared at the fish, tapping the chopstick on the glass. The fish, unfazed, continued to hold Dwayne's gaze.

'Looks lonely all by itself,' she said.

Dwayne shrugged. He pointed at a gold-embossed certificate beside the tank. 'Fancy-assed fish. Owners are probably sittin' on a goldmine there. Was thinking 'bout that the other day – gettin' meself a toucan or Komodo from Bali.'

Kaz fought back a laugh. *There were no toucans in Bali.* But now that Dwayne had his back to the tank, the fish moved closer to the glass. She watched as it hovered, its mouth opening and closing like a slow-motion scream.

When the waiter brought the spring rolls to the table, Dwayne bowed his head. 'Good job, mate,' he said, squinting at his badge. 'Wu, is it?'

'Correct.' Wu said. His uniform reminded Kaz of an airline attendant's, garish colours of orange and gold.

'Wu, like the Wu-tang clan,' Dwayne said.

'Love Wu-Tang,' Wu said, smiling in a way that Kaz wasn't entirely convinced.

'See that fish, Wu?' Wu nodded. 'What do ya call that, where you're from?'

'Aro-wa-na. Very smart fish. Carnivorous.'

Dwayne drummed the glass. 'We wanna eat it, Wu.'

He pulled his wallet out, counting out a wad of fifties. It was enough to pay for the trip to Bali they'd been planning for years.

'What are you doing?' Kaz hissed.

'You know dollars, Wu?'

'Not for sale. Rare this fish. See, even has certificate.'

'Yeah Wu, that's real impressive. But I want it on my plate.' In a pathetic gesture of chivalry, that Kaz recognised as fake, Dwayne continued: 'It's makin' me girlfriend uncomfortable.'

Kaz squirmed. The fish seemed to be studying Dwayne's hand movements through the glass.

'This fish been here for many years. Part of family. Very wise.'

'A fish don't know shit, mate. Except for fuckin' other fish and eating fish food.' She watched as Dwayne bit down on a spring roll. 'Get me the manager, Wu.'

Wu bowed and slunk away, smiling meekly at Kaz.

'You can't eat it, Dwayne,' she seethed. 'You can't just buy your way out of everything you know.' But he could. He'd bought her out every time they'd fought and fucked, luring her back with chocolates and gifts of crotchless pants. She stood up. *This was it. Time to take a fucking stand.* 'It's...' Everyone was staring at her – Dwayne, the whole restaurant, the fish too. But the words were caught in her throat. 'It's dumb.'

He stood up, towering over her. 'You think you know what's good for this fish?' She sunk back in her chair.

Wu and the owner returned: 'I sell for one thousand, five hundred. No less. You buy, I throw in a bottle of red. Deal?'

Dwayne grinned. 'Done.'

She watched as the fish did another lap of the tank, then stopped. Its eye was dark and bottomless. Was it winking at her – or blinking? She couldn't tell.

Her phone pinged. She glanced at a photo of the fish on Dwayne's plate, its tail hanging limp. A wedge of lemon beside its head.

Shud I batter it, babe?

Kaz didn't reply.

At 7am the next morning, Kaz got a call from the Mater Hospital. A nurse in Intensive Care. 'Dwayne's very ill. You need to come in urgently, he's been asking for you.'

Kaz blinked. 'This is a joke, right?'

'I'll put him on.'

She could hearbreathing, shallow and raspy. 'Dwayne?'

'F-f-f-f-f...'

'What?'

'Fa-fa-fa...'

'What?'

'F-f-f-FISH!'

'Now is not the time to think about that bloody fish! I'll be there soon, alright?'

But there was no response. Kaz grabbed her keys, thinking it was just like fucking Dwayne to die on her, before she had the chance to break up with him.

The doctor reminded Kaz of one of those from the TV soaps – dark hair, blue eyes, white coat, too good-looking to be true. 'Your husband is something of a medical anomaly.'

'Boyfriend,' Kaz corrected, 'Soon to be ex.'

'Indeed,' the Doctor said, nodding gravely at Dwayne. 'It's only a matter of time.'

She could barely recognise Dwayne, his skin a strange yellow green. As she stepped closer to the bed, she could see that it was peeling off in thick sheets. His stomach was huge and swollen, the hospital sheet rising like a tent.

'Is he contagious?'

The Doctor shook his head. 'You can hold his hand if you like.'

Kaz stepped back. 'Nah, it's ok.'

'Your husband ingested a rare type of fish. I don't know how to say this Karen, but we detected two separate heartbeats.'

'Huh?' Kaz stared at Dwayne's distended stomach.

The doctor drew back the bed sheet and squeezed clear fluid onto Dwayne's belly, running a probe across it. 'Watch.' The doctor pointed at a monitor illuminating Dwayne's belly. He moved the probe back and forth, until she saw a flash of movement. The doctor stopped, pointing at a long and thin shadow. It swam back and forth.

'What the fuck is that?'

'The fish is alive in there.'

Kaz gripped the bed rail. 'What's it doing?'

'Unsure,' the doctor said. 'It seems that the fish is using his body as a host. But we'll run some more tests.'

Kaz wondered if she'd taken the wrong floor and ended up in the loony bin ward. 'Well, what do *you* know? You're a doctor, right?'

'We've got a specialist flying over from the U.S. This is a rare case. Your boyfriend is going to make medical history.' They glanced at Dwayne as he moaned. 'Everyone loves a good David and Goliath story. And here we have man versus *fish*.'

A massive media scrum camped outside the hospital. An American camping store had even offered her big bucks to use photos of Dwayne to promote their new range of fishing lures. She'd been tempted – the hospital bills were growing – but the doctors had advised her not to speak to anyone.

By the third week, Dwayne was unrecognisable. His facial features had disappeared, his skin silver, scaly. And he was shrinking. Six foot to two foot in less than a month. Three slits appeared on either side of his rib cage, the skin flapping open and closed as he breathed. Kaz sat beside Dwayne's bed, as a team of doctors debated their cause.

'They're gills,' she said, throwing her coffee cup into the bin. It landed with a loud clang.

'Impossible,' one of the doctors said.

'These are scales, not some rare skin condition.' She pulled a pack of cigarettes from her pocket, putting one to her lip. 'You retards. Can't you see? He's turning into a fucking fish.'

When she arrived at the hospital, a hundred journalists swarmed around her. She hustled her way through the crowd.

Kaz was thrown into more chaos as she entered the ward. A team of doctors gathered, and a man guarded Dwayne's door, dressed in army greens. She spotted the doctor from all those weeks back, his TV good looks. 'Come this way,' he said, leading her into a small room.

He instructed her to sit. 'They're transferring him so he can get more specialist treatment in London. You just need to sign this waiver, releasing him to the –'

'London!'

An aquarium. He'll have 24-hour monitoring and a team of scientists that will observe him for the rest of his life.'

Kaz was surprised as tears fell. Her hand shook, the pen hovering over the dotted line.

'I'm sorry, Kaz. He may not be much of a man anymore, but he could save mankind.'

'What?'

'Well, if we could all morph into fish, like Dwayne, the effects of climate change could be reversed in as little as twenty years. Scientists are speculating that Dwayne could save our planet.'

'Save our planet?'

'We'd significantly reduce our carbon emissions as fish. Dwayne's the answer our world's been looking for.'

Dwayne – a hero? She was the one who'd stood by him, while he morphed into fucking Nemo. 'Are you nuts?' She scribbled her signature on the form and flung it at the doctor. 'Have it. I'm done.'

When she got to the ground floor, the media circled again. A journo thrust a microphone into her face: 'Kaz, what's it like to have sex with a fish?' She felt like decking the dickhead. She'd be known as the freak's girlfriend forever. But one thought floated through her mind, the tentacles of possibility growing.

She peered out into the crowd, standing on her tippy toes. 'Anyone here from A Current Affair?'

From the back of the crowd a hand shot up, like a shark fin. The fin moved closer, parting the sea of journalists.

The cameras clicked, capturing the first time Kaz had smiled in months. 'Tracey Grimshaw,' she muttered, as she elbowed her way through the crowd to meet the anonymous hand, 'here we fucking come.'

Laundromat

Ellen Rodger

Not everyone at the laundromat was old, though many had missing teeth and others, like Edith, suffered the kind of diabetes that at first puffs you out then deflates you, so that you live in a costume of skin that seems full of water. The laundromat had a café, and I served milkshakes and ice cream, toasted sandwiches and hotdogs, soft food you could eat with no teeth. One regular wore a pink sweatshirt with the word Jesus covered in oil stains. Another turned up every morning with white squint marks around her lovely tanned face, smelling of urine and shouting her order. Two toasted cheese and tomato sandwiches and a pot of tea.

Edith, whose wrong foot, the uninjured foot, was resting up on a chair, said yes please, crisply, when I offered her a drink. She worked in the laundromat, and whenever I looked at her, I felt the transference of her heavy painkillers, like weighty pins and needles in my pelvis. Edith had a special case manager that assessed the laundromat for hazards, measuring the base of Edith's walking stick by tracing its circumference on a piece of paper. Edith flourished under the attention and looked normal to me for the first time, straightening up under her case manager's concern for her, talking sanely about the feelings in her foot, the way it felt like a fireball sometimes, and other times it felt numb.

The laundromat café had three square tables, and the lace curtains at the windows appeared as though there were misty trees behind them, but it was the clotheslines, blurred through white gauze. Most days Edith moved nothing except the hand that turned the pages of her Mills and Boon novellas, and I had to fold the washing she was meant to fold, folding myself into a little blanket of sedation as I squared and balanced everything perfectly before placing items in baskets to be picked up and taken home.

Thursday. I walked to the supermarket to buy detergent, hundreds and thousands, hotdog buns and milkshake syrups. I saw the man with the blue sports bag and the tattoo on his calf of a naked woman sitting on a barrel with open legs. The supermarket had a fake hot air balloon advertising its reopening. It was the biggest shop in a quadrangle of grey stones and dirt that sparkled amber with broken glass. The shopping centre was full of rubbish. The rubbish was so profuse you grew to respect it. The sun scoured and sanitised the rubbish, then blew it down the hill to the laundromat's backyard.

Edith often asked me if I drank, and when I said yes, she'd ask again to confirm it. Her face up close was full of hundreds of black dots, and I wondered if she shaved. She was wearing a scarf around her jaw to cradle a toothache, and its lurex thread glittered when she said that though she herself didn't drink, her kids were drinkers, and her ex-husband was a drinker. When she asked if I had any pets and I said no, she lost even more faith in me.

Edith had dogs. She had lots of dogs and loved them more than people, dressing them up in tutus, socks and overcoats that she brought into the laundromat to secretly wash with other people's washing. Bother-free said the speech bubble on her favourite dog's Winnie the Pooh coat. Every day her middle-aged son came into the laundromat to use our toilet, wobbling towards us through the carpark on his kid's bike. He had a bright blue cast on his arm from punching a door, and when he said hello to me, he curtsied formally and held out the wrong hand to shake, the one with the cast. I didn't want to touch it. He asked me for a hotdog, and I made it, feeling ashamed, the way I always did when I served hotdogs to men.

Kids untethered to school wandered through the carpark, and from the backyard I watched Edith through the window, fluffing the café curtains with her walking stick. She couldn't stop. She said it was to do with her mother's obsession with curtains. They had to be perfect. No one else could touch them.

There were marks all over the toilet seat when I went back inside. I went through two pairs of gloves, washing and wiping everything down, then washed the bins too, laying them out in the sun. The sky started on the ground out here, curving over you, suffocating the suburb, and all the houses faced the wrong way on the street, their features turned into their own backyards.

I picked up rubbish from around the clotheslines and found a torn off sole of a complicated sports shoe, black shoelaces coiled elegantly like dehydrated worms, empty envelopes from the Department of Family and Community Services. Edith barely moved. She talked again about her ex-husband and how he used to drink all the time, no he didn't hit her, he abused her though, he abused her verbally, he abused her every time he got drunk, which was every single night.

Her voice was almost soundless. I resisted listening harder. I didn't want to take everything in.

A man in a government truck drove up to the bus stop with the new timetable, but the perspex box had been torn from the bus stop shelter and he drove away. Flowerbeds flourished with white crumped paper, logos and brands faded to vintage pastels. The yellow grass was shorn by government lawnmowers. Curtains were drawn. The curtains were mostly sheets and blankets. No weapons on the bus, the bus driver said to a boy with a plastic gun.

Edith sat next to me and pulled a small religious book from her bag, opening it at a precise spot for me to read something about the meaning of the word kingdom. She'd been baptised as an adult and had had a hard time finding a swimming costume for her public declaration. She'd converted when a couple knocked on her door one night when her ex-husband was drunk. Before she joined the church, she said, she didn't have a name for god, after all, the word god is a label, like man or woman, not a name like Edith or mine.

Friday. A couple came in to do their washing and Edith couldn't take her eyes off them. The woman was larger than the man, and up close I saw that the skin on the corner of her eye was bleeding. The man was childlike and looked as though he was working off some kind of guilt just by being in the laundromat, as though he was there as recompense for something to do with the woman's eye.

Edith stood up to watch as the man performed tasks with just one hand, pulling wet clothes from the tub by single arms and legs as if to demonstrate his lack of commitment, then putting his hoodie on and pulling it off as he ate chocolate bars from our vending machine.

Edith bought a chocolate bar from the vending machine too. Unwrapping it, she said that most people didn't know it, but chocolate was actually good for diabetics. She talked about her diabetes with pride, her voice so loud she must have wanted the woman and man to take notice of her, and the pink part in her hair stood out, as though talking about her condition lit up a special part of her brain with neon serotonin.

Then she talked about her injured foot, saying she couldn't remember if the pins were still in it, but when they were in it, they got infected, and this seemed to satisfy her too. She said that her son had told her she wasn't allowed to injure herself like that again, and his injunction seemed to please her by placing her in the role of a child.

I made Edith a coffee. I tried to imagine her being served by one of her children. She said that when the accident happened, she stayed in bed for three months because she couldn't walk.

'How did you get to the bathroom?' I asked.

'Hopped,' she said.

'What about food?'

Edith didn't say anything. There was a strange mark on her nose, a nick filled with black, and I looked away from it, picked up her Mills and Boon novella, and flipped to the last page. The story was called City Doctor, and I read the final paragraph out loud, kind of mocking Edith. 'A twinkling blue light danced in his eyes, and he said, who said anything about leaving, and then his head came down and covered her mouth with a kiss.'

'What about food Edith?' I said again.

'My son would bring me something eventually,' she said.

I waited at the bus stop. Silence, then birds flew into it, and Edith's son rode around the corner on his kid's bike, half man half boy, his feet enormous on the pedals, unbalanced, wobbling, he couldn't seem to ride it in a straight line. He almost corrected himself, but then he toppled over onto the road, and I heard him cry, 'Ow,' a kid's exclamation of pain. The driver of a slow-moving car waited patiently for him to pick himself up, and he shouted at them, though they'd had nothing to do with him falling.

I didn't call out to Edith's son to ask if he was alright because he hadn't seen me. I leaned back, hiding myself inside the bus shelter, and paid attention to the rubbish on the ground. Bright blue end of a knotted balloon, turquoise deodorant bottle with its plastic dehydrated ball, empty packet of Winfield Blue cigarettes.

Don't let children breathe your smoke, said the message on the empty cigarette packet, and I looked closely at the accompanying photo, of a girl with large brown eyes lying in a hospital bed, a doctor adjusting the breathing apparatus over her nose and mouth.

When I looked up, Edith's son was on the other side of the road talking to the man with the blue sports bag. I closed my eyes and saw hundreds of black dots, and when they faded, I saw Edith as a kid, lying in a hospital bed, being cared for by the doctor with the twinkling blue light in his eyes.

Monday.

'Get up out of your chair Edith, I'm sick of doing your work,' I wanted to say when I saw her with her wrong foot resting up on a chair as usual, reading her Mills and Boon novella.

But I said, 'Tell me about your ex-husband, Edith. What did he used to do to you? How did he make your life so bad?'

Meet you Halfway

Belinda Hermawan

When I was nine, my dad thought he'd 'change things up' for the July school holidays by taking the family on a road trip. Mum muttered under her breath as she packed enough clothes to last us a few days: 'It won't change anything'.

On the way up from Sydney, dark sandstone barriers loomed on either side of the Pacific Highway. Much like the road, I too was the sunken middle; carved space between my brothers in the backseat. Luke was one year older and Foster three years younger than me. I kept my elbows tucked in as they reached over to punch each other/share chips/pass on the Game Boy/pull on each other's t-shirts.

I remained silent as my brothers played a game of 'I Spy'. Tried to listen for any words from Mum to Dad or vice versa. Nothing.

It was only when Dad mentioned stopping in Newcastle for lunch that I spoke up.

'Have we reached Victoria yet?'

Dad kept his eyes on the road ahead. 'Who's Victoria? Is that a mate of yours?'

'No, I mean like Melbourne. Where Nanna and Pop live.'

Mum glanced primly over her shoulder. She wasn't used to explaining things, and her voice went from pleasant to flaccid when she explained, 'Sweetie, we're going to the Gold Coast, which is in Queensland.'

My brothers were shouting 'rock, paper, scissors' in my ears, thrusting their decisions in front of my face.

'Yeah,' I said. 'How far until Victoria?'

At this, my brothers retracted their weapons, stared at me as if I'd offered to take over driving the station wagon.

'Victoria is below New South Wales, you num-nuts,' Luke said.

'Num-nuts,' Foster repeated.

I couldn't see Dad's face. The car swerved a little. A squiggle, like when you try to get a pen to work.

'Look at that, Jen,' Dad said to Mum. 'Such a Sydneysider, she hasn't even learnt where Melbourne is. Couldn't give a rat's arse.'

Mum didn't respond.

I was about to reach through the front seats to tug on her sleeve, to tell her I really hadn't learn about it in school, when two sets of scissors kept me in place.

I tell a version of this story to Geoff, the Head of HSIE, at lunchtime in the staffroom. Despite HSIE standing for Human Society & Its Environment, he has little patience for human interactions not aligned with his interests. I hope to be shooed away from his table after extracting an exasperated 'Yes' to my request.

'Renee,' he says, fingers pressing into his salami sandwich, the butter oozing, 'it's not like I'm asking you to teach History or Geography.'

'But I'd be useless on the Canberra trip,' I reply. 'I don't know anything about parliament or law-making.'

'Neither does the Prime Minister.'

I lean forward. He pulls back, as if I'm trying to steal a bite. 'Please. Send me out bush instead.'

'It's not my call,' he answers while chewing. 'It's the Vice Principal's.'

The Vice Principal claims all Year 9 homeroom teachers benefit from rotating excursion duties, but really it's about who gets to go on the ski trip. We're a state school in a high-SES area in Sydney; there have to be some perks. The Canberra HSIE Camp comes with two days of skiing at Perisher after all the learning, a relatively cheap option compared to where these kids are used to holidaying. The academically gifted kids pick Canberra. For those who are more outdoorsy, or whose parents grumble at having to spend a single cent more than the compulsory school fees, Bush Camp in the Blue Mountains is a given.

Only one parent kicked up a fuss about both options, and that's because she misread the HSIE Camp's focus on 'humanities' as 'humanitarian'. How dare we make her choose between a refugee camp and the wilderness? Little Johnny doesn't have the stomach for either.

Geoff has not given me the answer I want. I stand, the sight of the hardcourts outside reminding me of a duty swap advertised during staff briefing. 'Geoff, aren't you meant to be on duty for Jill?'

'Ha! It's high school. They'll be right.'

The Gold Coast's amusement parks were a blur of superheroes, water slides and fairy floss.

At Movie World, Foster cried because:

- He did not meet the height requirement for the Batman ride
- He had a last name for a first name and couldn't buy any personalised merchandise
- The shop assistant asked him if he was named after a bear and he

was scared of bears

It turns out the shop assistant was saying 'beer' in a Kiwi accent

Us kids hated beer, the empty cans on the table in the games room at home a sign that Dad had slept on the couch

Personally, I loved the 'Western Action' stunt show the most. Staged outdoors, it was the wild west in its sanitised movie set glory: cowboys with guns chasing each other, jumping off roofs, dangling from horses, kicking up sand. I remember looking up from the bleachers and thinking the sun resembled that of Foster's drawings –impossibly yellow, with rays extending to all corners. Luke and I wanted to see the show again, but Dad said we had a lot more to get to, including the *Gremlins* ride.

We didn't know it'd be the show's last year at Movie World. Neither did we know it'd be our last winter together as a family.

Years later I would wonder if all the adults had always known: 'turning over a new leaf' means turning over to a new page, a blank one. Anything drawn previously – the sun's warmth, for instance – is left behind.

I track down the Vice Principal, Barbara, after school. She's on duty out front in a hi-vis vest, refereeing the usual stand-offs between parents in SUVs who can't seem to get through the pick-up area without double-parking or cutting each other off.

'Are you for real?' she shouts at anyone who'll listen, throwing her hands in the air. 'Oh, so you can get through a Maccas drive-thru with no trouble, but you can't manage here?'

The only people listening are me, a cluster of Year 10 boys, and maybe a seagull or two.

'Barb, I don't like Canberra,' I plead.

'Nobody *likes* Canberra,' she replies, hands now on hips. 'Did you know Melbourne was Australia's capital until 1927? It's only because we called bullshit that they were like "fine, we'll meet you halfway" and then we all ended up with a garbage tip three-hundred-and-eighty kilometres closer to us than to them. Did you know that?'

'I did know that, actually.'

'See, you PE teachers are more than just running around and playing games.' I suspect she's winked at me behind her big black sunglasses. 'Look, you've been on Bush Camp three years in a row. No swapsies.'

I open my mouth to protest but catch sight of a changeover occurring. Court-ordered. Johnny getting into an Audi to spend half the week with his dad. I've spent countless hours this year repeating the same messages to both of his parents because they don't communicate, generally treating instructions like they're the lolly selection at the local deli: pick and mix.

I jump at the sound of a car backfiring. It turns out it's not a car.

'Oi!' Barbara roars, turning to our right. 'You think I can't see you Year 8s jumping on poppers? Detentions tomorrow for the lot of you!

My mum used to call poppers 'Primas,' which is apparently what they called them in Victoria when she was at school. I knew everything had changed permanently when she ordered us three 'juice boxes' at a café in Canberra, as if she was on holiday and wanted to make sure the foreigners understood her.

I slurped on my popper, clutching the carton and continuing to suck even when there was nothing left but a gurgling sound. This was exactly my feeling at being brought down to the capital to visit her on the September/ October school holidays. The Gold Coast was an incalculable distance away; over a year ago, multiplied by all the disappointments since.

The Floriade flower festival was boring. All tulips, en masse. Yellow here, purple there, pink, red, boring. We trudged around the clay-coloured paths, stepping on her footprints. It was another ominous sign: when you're responsible for children, whether they're yours by blood or by the education system, you don't let them walk behind you. You drop back and make sure you can see them.

Finally, one of us snapped.

'If Melbourne is so good,' Luke shouted at her back, 'then why aren't we down there right now? Are you ashamed of us or what? How about Nanna and Pop? Do they still love us?'

She whipped around but didn't stop walking, legs ticking over backwards. Her face was a tulip; slender and poised. Pretty, when in season.

When a kid has a go at you, you don't react with pretty. You tell them where it's at, 'it' being the place kids are supposed to be.

I don't remember what she said. To this day, Foster reckons she didn't say anything. Luke only remembers wanting to push her into a pond.

Overnight, I receive emails from both of Johnny's parents, each telling me the same thing: I should choose the camp he'll attend. Even though they've agreed for once, it reeks of laziness.

I'm angry for Johnny. I'm angry for every kid who gets sent to school to be raised by teachers before going home and being routinely ignored.

I read out the notices at the start of homeroom: full school assembly this morning, and a reminder about donations for the P&F bake sale. Johnny approaches after I'm done. The rest of the kids busy themselves with their smartphones.

Johnny is not really Little Johnny anymore. He is in a growth spurt, though he tends to shrink when talking to his other teachers. He sighs and says, 'Miss, just pick whatever's quieter.'

His parents' divorce must've been loud, unlike my parents' where actions did the talking. My dad didn't think he could appeal anyway. In his words, he was a tail-ender prone to being dismissed LBW – once the finger went up, it was back to the pavilion.

I try to give him an honest assessment. 'Hmm. Canberra has politicians arguing, and there'll be a lot of history talks. Bush Camp will have a lot of shouting from the teachers, sometimes at each other.'

'Which one are you going on?'

'Canberra. But you should think about what you want. Some kids don't have a choice. You know what that's like, right? To not have a say?'

He bites his lip as he mulls it over. 'I guess I want to try skiing,' he finally says with a shrug.

'All right. But at least take the opportunity to learn some stuff for HSIE, you got me?' I think of his report card. 'I know you're smarter than that C.'

'Aw, Miss. It's so boring though. PE is the only fun subject.'

'You're not wrong, Johnny. It's just that sometimes you've got to suck it up and push through.'

He pulls a face. 'And about the bake sale, Miss…'

'I'll take care of it. I'm going to have buy a truckload of cakes with the excuses I'm hearing from this homeroom. I don't want to be lectured by the P&F president.'

'You're the best,' he says quickly before rushing away.

While browsing the bakery section of Coles after school, I catch sight of the flower display by the entrance. Amongst the choices are bunches and bunches of tulips. Yellow, pink, red. Too much of something pleasant is still bitter to me, much like over-steeped tea.

I have a brief thought about replying to Mum's texts from two months ago, her casual words not referencing the pain.

I'm not there yet, but maybe one day I'll inch to halfway.

Mistress of Her Destiny

Claudia Ellen King

Early afternoon sun beamed off the ocean of nasturtiums that bobbed and weaved, like schools of effervescent fish, in the overgrown lawn. Even from the kitchen, elbows deep in unclogging the drain, I smiled at their gaudy brightness and the woody smell of the soil. Nathan, my partner, was out there with a spade, digging a garden bed. A gnarled lemon tree grumbled in the corner. It had shed its spring coat of hard white blossoms a week earlier. A few days of relentless dew, heat, and intrepid insects, had trampled the little flowers into the ground. The tree remained fruitless, despite my best efforts.

Actually, that might be an overstatement. A best effort would have looked something like a deep Google search into year-round treatment for lemon trees that have gone barren at an early age. A trip to Bunnings, or my Dad's, wouldn't have gone amiss. But I opted for the labour intensive approach of peeing on it at every chance I got.

I still don't have any lemons. But really, the garden wasn't my responsibility. It was supposed to be Nathan's. I had watched him, giddy with the joy of signing our first lease, declare his plans for a flourishing veggie patch that would be feeding us within a month. He dug a six metre square garden bed, loaded it with compost, and then left it for a year. Its morphing stages of decomposition, when I look back, were an apt reflection of our disintegrating relationship.

Let's plunge into the hallowed realm of academia for a moment, since I've found that a few women have gone a long way to explaining the forces behind that festering garden bed. In her essay *Young Women and Housework,* Joanne Baker articulates, 'In a post- feminist climate it is clearly harder for young women to identify patterned, systemic inequality. If located at all, inequality tends to be understood as the failure of the individual who is now understood to be empowered and, in Chilla Bulbeck's (2005) words, 'mistress of her destiny'.'

If you need a little jargon update, a post-feminist climate would be a world in which:

It is a presumption (perpetuated by mainstream culture) that women and men have achieved basic equality and, thus, can collectively move on from feminism.

As such, a woman has control over the power dynamics in her relationships with men.

The movement is championed by pop-cultural representations of young, single, heterosexual, urban, sassy women.

I uncovered Baker's paper during a rage research, following a particularly gag-inducing clean of a refrigerator. I had been thinking about these issues for a while - four to eight hours a week, in fact, since I timeshared my pondering with chores, university and work. A question that kept popping up was whether I simply expected far too much. If I was hoping that Nathan would try and meet my standards, then was he not similarly furious at my resistance to his lackadaisical approach to domesticity?

None of the tidying gurus had anything to say about it. The infamous Marie Kondo didn't intersperse her (life-changing) folding technique with a commentary on the forces underpinning the resistance of the male species to housework. Eve Rodsky, author of *Fair Play,* with her rules for equalising home duties, teeters around the edge of penetrating how (dear god) books still need to be published on this issue. In her recent TIME article she quips, 'My husband is a smart, caring guy. So why was it so hard for him to understand and appreciate how much extra work I was doing to benefit our family and him… Then it hit me: lists don't work; but systems do.'

Let's take a moment to reflect on an interesting little structure that she deploys in this argument. What comes first is a pre-emptive defence of the man that she has chosen to share her life with. Next, we are hit with her bafflement at his inability to empathise and change his behaviour. Finally, we have a system (designed and put in place by her, the already overburdened woman) to attempt to guide the well-meaning man towards a resolution of this conflict.

These patterns of dialogue are symptomatic of a culture in which the fault is placed on women for getting themselves into situations of inequality. This drops us straight into the middle of a fully-fledged Catch-22. The impacts of domestic inequality are felt most deeply by women. The issue is a multi-headed hydra of socio-political forces. Systems designed to change male behaviour, however, tend to place women in the position of responsibility for fixing the problems. Understanding this issue, let alone fixing it, is really, fucking complicated.

Nathan and I were heading down South a while back. He was lounging behind the wheel of our mate's Troopie van. He's not a blokey guy but when it comes to Royal Enfields and Troop Carriers, he gets this dopey, slack-jawed expression. We'd arrived in Goulburn and, after scouting out the town's selection of bakeries, decided to eat our supply of mixed nuts and keep driving.

'If you spot the bananas, that'd be amazing,' he flicked the words over his shoulder.

I heaved through boxes and backpacks. My butt was jammed against the side windows and I was using one of my legs to hold back our mattress. There's something about tight spaces that makes my body feel enormous, like a heifer forced into a steel contraption, teats bulging with milk. I know that sounds a bit absurd, but honestly, it's how I feel when I have to squeeze into things. My psychologist told me that the words I use to describe my self-image would, in another context, perfectly depict a troll from a children's novel.

I found the mixed nuts, plus a couple of apples, and hauled myself back into the passenger seat. Nathan was already in gear and we rolled onto the main road that stretched, uncomfortably wide, through the centre of Goulburn.

'You know, I've been noticing how we manage things on holidays,' his voice wandered with the road, 'I feel like our division of work is really equal. I know you did so much yesterday, you know, to get us ready. And now I'll drive all day to get us there. So we both end up doing a really fair amount of work.'

'Mhm.'

Let me introduce you to a little concept called mental load, which my dear man was not aware of at the time of his statement. He is well versed in the topic now. The mental load, when used in reference to domestic tasks, describes the way that labour becomes exponentially more tiring when an individual is also carrying out the scheduling, anticipation, and (sometimes) delegation of tasks. I'll give you an example.

The 'day before' that Nathan referred to was the culmination of a weeks worth of planning. I'll spare you the full autopsy and stick with some choice slices of gore. (Feel free to listen to the William Tell Overture while reading this bit, I think it really helps with the tone.)

Organise for Nathan to transfer me the money so I can buy all of the groceries for the trip; make sure Nathan knows what time to pick friend's van up; check that rent's pre-paid; clean the kitchen so the cockroaches don't get any worse; submit final assessment for uni project; shop at Aldi to get what you can cheaply; shop at Woolworths for everything else; pre-cook and freeze a stew in separate containers to keep the esky cold (bugger, remember to pick up esky from Mum and Dad's); download directions to campsite and print a copy as backup – printer breaks – timeshare drive to Officeworks with phone-call to landlord to reschedule inspection that clashes with trip.

A bit much? I know. But you either thought, 'Jesus, this is my life, I don't want to hear it!' or your thought, 'This woman needs to give it a rest.' Either way, I've proved my point. Inequity remains. Give me a car and a long highway any day.

After eighteen months together, nine in the same house, Nathan and I stood either side of the dining room as he told me that he was going to dinner with an old friend of his. He wasn't being unreasonable. There was nothing wrong with what he wanted in that moment. But I had reached the end of a day, not unlike the one before our road trip, and I heard my partner tell me that he was committing his leisure time, the nice time, to someone who had not pulled his pubic hair out of the shower drain earlier that morning.

I picked up my phone and I threw it. I was aiming for the kitchen door. I've always had terrible aim. Wildly off its intended course, the phone missed Nathan's ear by about an inch. It left two holes in the wall: one from the initial impact, deep enough to jam a thumb into, and a second from the spin on the thing, where it took another chunk out of the plaster.

'This is over.' There wasn't much expression in his voice as he walked out the door.

I'm the first to acknowledge double standards. If he, a man, had thrown a phone at me, the consequences could have been much worse. I benefited, in the aftermath, from a swathe of people brushing off my violence as a moment of irrationality. When I recounted the story, the almost unanimous response was, 'We all do crazy things.'

This is where it gets a bit muddy. Physical aggression is abuse. I would tell any friend of mine to stay far away from a perpetrator, which I guess I am. But Nathan, a month later, found me. He asked me to explain what had happened. For almost two years, he had responded to my requests for help in the kitchen by telling me to not 'mother'. He owed me over a thousand dollars because he never did the grocery shopping, and would often forget to split the receipts that I'd leave on the kitchen bench. He still hadn't planted a single tomato vine or lavender bush in the garden bed.

Now, it is six months later. We live in separate houses. Yesterday, in the car, he organised my glove box while I was driving. I hadn't asked him to do it. The week before, he turned up to my home with a box of veggies to cook dinner, and cleaned up afterwards. It took a demonic transformation on my part, an act of unhinged rage, to illuminate the unacceptable burden that partnered living places on the shoulders of women. I know it's not just me. Studies have repeatedly indicated that single women are happier than married women, and that the opposite applies to men. My Mum volunteered the idea that we could cut laziness from the species by refusing to breed with the paternal lines that exhibit this trait. Clearly, neither of us has the answer. I can't help but see, however, a tenuous thread of connection stretching out in front of me.

As I write this, two weeks have passed since an all female panel on the ABC's Q&A generated a shockwave that would make you think a tectonic plate had shifted underneath Australia. Controversy exploded over the following statement by the show's guest, Mona Eltahawy, 'How long must we wait for men and boys to stop…murdering us? How many rapists must we kill until men stop raping us?' In the days following, the cowardly ABC removed the episode from I-view. But I have watched, overjoyed, as conversations exploded. Death and violence are devastating forces, but when Eltahawy invoked the power of the word 'kill,' people started listening. When I lobbed a hard metal object (not-directly) at a man, he started listening.

Is it any wonder that, sometimes, it's so tempting to burn things?

More river

Zoe Deleuil

Without Frank, there's no money for Bali this year. So I rang my brother and arranged to pick up the keys for the shack at Moore River.

The kids found their bedroom and argued happily over who got the top bunk, while I opened the back door and stood on the verandah. From there, you could see the point at which the tannin-brown river almost met the wild grey sea, separated by a fragile sandbar.

My grandmother used to bring me here, with her friend Mia and Mia's grandson, Lee. I remember his white surfer's hair, his eyes half-closed in the sun. All my memories of him were on the beach, up close. Sometimes we paddled in the tea-water river, other times we ran down to the shore and let the waves terrify us. We didn't know each other in Perth, so when we said goodbye at the end of the holiday that was it.

He's a real estate agent now, selling prime coastal property. I see his face on billboards, those same blue eyes, that same fine blonde hair, when I drive along the West Coast Highway.

Moore River is near unchanged as a holiday destination, a quiet and self-contained settlement with a library in a static caravan that opens for two hours on Saturday mornings. I've always felt that there's a kind of spirit to it, a distinct energy at the exact point where the sleepy river almost touches the vast churning grey of the sea.

Of course, it has a shameful history. In the 1920s a settlement for Aboriginal people was established, away from the beach and the river mouth, a kind of orphanage, prison, halfway house for the broken and stolen. It's cruel, how the settlers chose the most picturesque places – Rottnest, Fremantle, Moore River – to build their jails.

In the evening we wandered down to the caravan park to meet up with my friend Annette and her family. The kids came without complaint, probably wanting, like me, to get away from the holiday house we couldn't quite fill with only the three of us. Tom was grubby and probably hungry, Stella was eager to please, greeting Annette and Dennis.

It was peak hour at the camp kitchen. Men in short sleeves commandeered the barbecues, while the women were in the kitchen, fiddling with feta and iceberg lettuce.

Wine was needed. I took a bottle of chardonnay from my Esky, poured Annette and me two generous glassfuls, then wandered back out to the barbecues, which surrounded a central outdoor dining area. Every tray was crammed with meat, the steaks sweating beads of blood, the lamb chops sizzling in their own young fat and the sausages spitting and rolling, shiny and flecked with black. All except for one barbecue, which was crowded with crayfish, red and ugly, like enormous prehistoric pests from the bottom of the ocean, where personally I think they should have stayed.

'Sailed to Rotto to catch these,' the cook announced to anyone within long earshot.

'You must really like them,' I commented.

'I'm allergic to them,' he replied, and I noticed he was looking a bit swollen and patchy around the eyes. 'Just do it for everyone else.'

At times like this, and it's not something I'm proud of, I reflect that Frank was not the obvious choice for an untimely departure.

'Hope he's got an Epi-pen on standby,' I said to Dennis under my breath.

'He'll need more than an Epi-pen in a minute,' Dennis muttered back. 'He's practically purple.'

We both looked away, trying not to laugh, and I had an unfamiliar feeling, something I recognised but hadn't felt for a long time. Anticipation. Of more laughs, more banter about nothing much. Like the night was something to be enjoyed, not just tolerated until it was late enough to go to bed.

'I'll do the meat,' I said to Dennis, picking up the tongs before he could stop me. 'I always do it.'

He looked surprised, tried to shake his head and take the tongs from me, but I held onto them and after a silent struggle he gave up. Every night I cooked in our kitchen. Why, when it's public, when there's glory to be had, when it's meat, should it be any different?

After a while Stella materialised from wherever she'd been playing and stood on the lawn before us, solemn and delicate in her denim shorts and began turning cartwheels. Dennis watched her, sipping his beer slowly, standing with his head slightly tipped back and his eyes narrowed like he was on the deck of his own yacht and not standing in some grotty caravan park camp kitchen. She caught his eye, smiling and hopeful.

'She's a skinny little thing, isn't she?' he remarked to me. 'Nothing on her at all.'

And I felt sad. She was only nine. You really don't get much time, as a person in a girl's body, before you start getting sized up and commented on.

Next to me, he kept watching her and she kept looking at him in between cartwheels and I thought of how much I wanted to keep her for myself.

We've been invited here, I reminded myself. Annette is your friend. Don't get into a fight.

Frank would have understood why it bothered me, once I'd outlined it to him. He was always the person I could rant to. Usually in bed with the lights off, maybe a sleeping child tucked between us, our secret place where I could debrief, get it out, and then forget about it. But he wasn't here. As soon as the sonographer said we'll just scan your chest, to see if it's gone any further – he was on his way, getting smaller and more distant until one day there were only three of us.

The flies were becoming unbearable. It was as if they were drawn to me, as though my thoughts were seeping out of my skin.

As it got darker, I looked out into the night, wondering where the place was beyond here, the old settlement, all those unmarked graves in the darkness. The image of Frank's coffin came back to me – a hideous thing covered in lurid white lace, and I pictured it in our living room, taking up all available space. Something we were always tripping over, something we didn't know how to get around.

And then the laughter got louder, and the smell of the crayfish and the volume rising as the blokes started in on their fourth or fifth beers were all of a sudden closing over me like a wave I couldn't quite get under in time.

And Dennis was moving closer, right up to my ear, so I could feel his breath, and he was saying, you know, you can always come over to visit, the kids and Ann are away next weekend, you could come over and cocoon at ours for a bit. Watch a movie or something. As he handed me the tray for the cooked meat his thumb stroked mine, so softly it could have been an accident.

The meat was cooked and I started to load it onto the tray he'd brought me, helpfully, and I wondered, did I imagine that? After all, I've sometimes been called a bit of a thinker, which is not considered a compliment around here.

As I took the meat off the tray I felt myself getting flustered. Was I supposed to clean the barbecue? I didn't know the etiquette, because I should have been in the kitchen with all the other women.

I picked up Dennis's beer and poured it over the metal tray and instantly the hot steam rose up and seared my bare arm as efficiently as if I'd laid it flat against the metal. I should have known that would happen, should have remembered that most basic physics lesson of hydrogen bonds being broken by heat.

'How's it going?' I said to Annette. She would have burn cream with her, a fully stocked medical kit, but I couldn't admit what I'd done. Annette would not barbecue, and therefore she would not get burned. She knew her place, and made it her own with grace, and part of me longed to still be like her.

'Good. Let's get a table, shall we?' She moved over to a man who was sitting at one of the tables. 'Right. There's seven of us here ready to eat so you'll need to move up a bit,' she told him, clattering down plates and cutlery and clearing her throat a few times. After a brief standoff he gave up the table and quietly moved on.

'Oh, I didn't mean for you to go! But thanks. Kids! Dinner!'

There they were, just how I liked them, with bare feet and grubby faces, ready for food and bed.

I'll wash them back at the house, and they'll fall asleep like wild creatures caught by their tangled sheets. Tom flaps himself to sleep. As a newborn he would pump his little arms up and down until he wore himself out. Even now, he'd go from tossing, rolling and jumping to still in a second. It was as if, once he had discharged every last bit of energy, he switched himself off. Stella would lie awake for hours, only giving in when she was squared away next to me.

'We'll get going after dinner, hey, kids?'

'Okay,' they replied in unison, with what I knew was relief disguised as fake reluctance. They needed the escape of sleep as much as I did. They would lose themselves in play, in books, in screens, but then I'd find them sitting somewhere, very still, and I'd see what this was really like for them, that kids don't just bounce back like people kept telling me they did.

Later, I lay on the sagging mattress, Stella beside me, my grandmother's rose-patterned cotton sheets light across my legs, my arm burning.

'Do you still like coming here?' said Stella.

I turned to her and kissed her smooth, flat forehead.

'I like being here with you.'

And for once, she closed her eyes and fell asleep, her breathing deep and steady beside me. As I lay there listening to her, I thought, we will never really know this place.

Perhaps the closest I came to knowing its true spirit was when I was here as a child with Lee. That simple happiness of playing on the beach while the land and the sea held us. Everything gets blurry once you get older.

The humming of something beneath the waves, something close and troubled here that will never be quiet until there is healing, some kind of restoration that no one seems to want to talk about.

So often, I wish that there were something more I could do. But I don't know what. You can only try, listen, learn. Hope for more understanding. More ocean, more river. More money. More time.

Maybe that's why we try so hard to ignore the history of these places. Because if we did, we'd have to admit that we don't really belong here.

Or maybe it's just me. Maybe I'm not well. Maybe on Monday I'll put on my non-mad clothes, go to the doctor and ask for something to help me sleep. And before I go, I'll do my face nicely with the makeup the girl at the chemist showed me how to apply.

Just blend, she said. Her own makeup was perfectly blended, her tanned skin smooth as paint, her eyes enhanced by a perfect little flourish on each side, drawn on with eyeliner, and expertly blended. Whenever you feel like your makeup isn't quite right, just keep blending, she said. You blend and blend and then blend some more.

Nail House

Sean Wilson

I don't venture out much these days. I stay indoors, finishing a cross-stitch by the front window or else napping in the sunroom beside the hydrangeas and devil's ivy. I stay out of the back yard for the most part. It's a tangle of white lantana and purple phlox, with an old yellow gum looming over it all. Then there's the issue with the apartment building windows on all sides. Each long, flat face of building with tens of these blinking square eyes all pointing down into the garden. It's like cold, grey grandstand seating, wrapping around the grass and leaves and flowers. An awful, permanent audience.

No, I don't much like being in the back these days.

The neighbourhood isn't what it used to be. When Roy and I first moved in, all those years ago, there were corner stores selling flour in parcels, fresh meat wrapped in butcher's paper, jam jars with wax paper on top. There were small hardware stores where you could buy a hammer that would last a lifetime. There were dressmakers who would take the time to talk to you about your life, about your health, while they ran measuring tape down your flank. Life was easy and it was slow. You felt like a part of the neighbourhood and you sensed that the neighbourhood made up part of you.

These days, I walk the streets and I hardly recognise the place. The drapery store where I bought fabric for our tablecloths is now a cafe where they sell poached eggs covered with strange leafy vegetables. The old bank where my friend Judy worked as a teller is now the offices of yet another real estate firm, the fifth in walking distance. The post office that for decades was our link to the outside world is now a bar where they serve colourful cocktails. Young people stream out of its doors to drink at the tables out front. They take out their little phones and take photographs of each other posing with the cocktails. They check the photographs on the phone screen and then they do it all again, the same pose, the same cocktail, all under the watchful eyes of men wearing black clothes and lanyards.

I used to have a dog for company. When you have a dog, you get out more. There's a reason to step out into the street, to walk around the block, waiting every now and then while the dog sniffs a tree or a fence. Penny, my little terrier, died on Good Friday three years ago. After the grief of the loss had dulled a little, I remember thinking how strange it was for her to die on that day. Of all days, to die on Good Friday.

I buried her out beside the lantana. I almost expected to see her again that Sunday, yapping at the back door like nothing had happened. It doesn't work like that, not these days when everything is studied and measured. There's no magic like that anymore.

I get a knock at the door. I'm asleep in the sunroom when it happens and the sound drags me out of a dream. In the dream, Roy is alive and well and driving us to the beach on a warm summer day, the sun turning the light hairs on his forearms into shimmering gold.

I'm rubbing my eyes and cursing under my breath when I get to the door. I pull it open to find a young man dressed in a navy suit and a deep red tie. He's standing on my porch, smiling from ear to ear.

'Hello,' he says. 'Sorry to bother you but do you have a couple of minutes to chat?'

A tram rumbles by on the street behind the young man. A mechanic pushes a silver sports car into the tyre shop across the road. A magpie lands on the roof of the fitness building, with its singlet-wearing patrons running in place behind the windows. It's bright and it's hot and it's all incredibly noisy.

'That depends,' I say, staring into the young man's eyes. 'What are you selling?'

'Nothing at all,' he says. 'In fact, I was hoping you'd be the one interested in selling.'

I should've known. I'd been drowsy from the dream with Roy. I should've tallied the smile and suit and leather-bound portfolio in his hand and added it up in my head.

'Oh,' I say. 'You're one of them?'

The young man shuffles his polished shoes on the porch. He glances past me, into the hallway, his eyes taking in all the angles and his brain making quick calculations.

'I'm afraid so,' he says. 'My name's Amir.'

'You know you're not the first person to stand at my door and make a pitch, don't you?'

Amir looks over his shoulder as a young couple walk their greyhound past us in the street. They each carry matching tote bags on their shoulders, beige in colour with black block letters on the side. Their heads are titled down, eyes fixed on the phones in their hands. They walk on like this, the young couple, not looking where they're going, not looking at the world around them. They stare down at their phones like characters from that myth, watching their own reflection.

'I'm sure you've had a few visitors over the years,' says Amir. 'I hope you don't mind one more?'

There's a way he asks this that reminds me of Roy. There's a cheekiness to it, a boldness. It's insistent but it's not presumptuous. It puts me at ease. I was about to send him on his way and close the door but I hesitate. I hold him in my gaze.

'Well,' I say, 'you might as well say what you came here to say.'

Amir smiles. He shuffles his portfolio from one hand to the other and clears his throat.

'I work for a boutique developer,' says Amir. 'We don't make those soulless, massive apartment complexes with those ugly, prefab concrete faces. I'm sure you've seen them popping up around here.'

I nod. Amir shakes his head.

'Of course,' he says. 'You've got one next door. Well, we're different. We create luxury, small-scale developments. The units in our properties are large. They're made for families and they have charm and the right kinds of amenities. Our developments are smart and they fit in with the surroundings, rather than impose themselves on them.'

I notice some dandruff on the shoulder of Amir's suit. I have an urge to reach out and brush it away for him. I feel like a mother at that moment. Protective. He notices me looking at him but he continues on with his speech like a train on rails.

'We don't work with slimy real estate agents,' says Amir. 'We're not interested in squeezing every dollar out of every square metre. We do the hard work ourselves. We do our research. We look out for overlooked properties or nail houses like this and we approach the owners ourselves.'

'Nail houses?' I ask. 'What do you mean by that?'

Amir's eyes open wide. He crosses his legs so that he's putting most of his weight on one foot.

'It's a sort of saying in the industry. It's silly,' says Amir. 'A nail house is a kind of holdout, I guess, when there's gentrification going on. It sort of sticks out like a nail that's been halfway hammered into a piece of wood. It's a stupid saying, really.'

I stare at Amir. I look him up and down, from his pointy black shoes to his expensive suit and perfectly tied tie. I look at his teeth, too-white and pulled into a straight, perfect line like a seam in trousers.

'I'm sorry to disappoint you, Amir,' I say, barely hiding the anger in my voice, 'but I'll be going before this house does.'

Amir clears his throat again. He opens his portfolio and glances down at some papers before looking up at me.

'Maybe your husband would like a chat sometime,' says Amir, 'or maybe your son or daughter? I'd be happy to go over our proposal. I'm sure there'd be something attractive in there. You know, the zoning has changed since you would've bought this place and the opportunity to do something good with the land, to help some families get a really good quality place are really attractive. Of course, you'd be well compensated for making that happen.'

'My husband Roy is dead. He's been gone ten years and we never had children,' I say. I look over Amir's shoulder and watch three men in orange vests carry steel wire from a truck toward a construction site. The men curse as the edge of the wire drags on the ground, screeching as it goes. 'This is my house and I won't let it go the way of the rest of the neighbourhood. Not while I have any say in it. I think you better leave now. I don't think we'll be able to help each other.'

'Okay then,' says Amir. He reaches into the breast pocket of his suit and pulls out a small card. He holds it up in my direction. 'In case you change your mind.'

'I won't,' I say, shaking my head.

Amir smiles and then turns and walks out into the street

Later, in the evening, I decide to take a walk around the block. The air has that cool feeling of late spring and I have the image from the dream in my mind, of the drive and Roy's hair glowing in the sun. I feel the need to be outside, a feeling I rarely get these days. It's as if I'm trying to finish the dream, to help it reach a conclusion. As if I'm trying to catch on to it like a wave and ride it back to shore.

I move slowly on our street, the high street, past bicycles locked up to street signs and small, snub-nosed cars parked end-to-end as far as I can see. I walk past the store where I used to buy perfume that's now a co-working studio, according to the sign in the window. I walk past the chemist that Angelo and his wife Carmela used to run, where we used to buy cough medicine and aspirin. Now it's full of colourful dresses with odd, asymmetrical patterns on every piece of fabric. I walk past the store where we bought our first fridge. Today, it's a thrift store run by the Salvation Army.

This is my paradise and it's slowly fading like a photograph on the wall. Every time I walk this street, it's changed a little more.

I turn a corner and walk with the breeze at my back. I put my hand out and grab hold of railing and fence posts at the front of homes. I let them carry some of my weight as I move along the street. Seven or eight houses down, I stop and stare at a large, cream-coloured bungalow. It's Beth and Ian's place. Only, it's not their place anymore. There's a sleek, black car in the driveway. There are scooters and bikes and footballs on the porch. There's a brand-new trampoline covered on all sides by mesh that looks like a cage.

I close my eyes and stand in front of the house. In front of Beth and Ian's house. I see myself standing here, holding a dish filled with baked potatoes and onion and cream. Roy is by my side. He's smoking a cigarette, puffing quickly as he opens the gate. He stubs it out on the tree in front of the house as we walk up the path. We reach the entrance and he wraps an arm around me as he lifts his other arm and knocks over and over and over on the door listening for the people we know.

Pull The Other One

Ann Erskine

Gran was on the verandah in a canvas-backed chair by the card table with Rabbie Burns, her Scottie, at her feet.

The Harbour shimmered with too-bright shards of light and Susannah's dazzled pupils shrivelled in defiance. She put a hand up to shade her face, dragged over another chair, positioned it next to Gran, and let herself subside into it.

Fixated on the form guide, Gran grunted and waved a hand. 'Just got to check this one out. A little mare, she's a stayer.' She crinkled her nose. 'Don't like the look of the jockey, though.'

It was Greek to Susannah. All she knew were the envelopes she handed over to Bob, the local SP bookie, at the corner store.

Gran clamped,her teeth over the end of her pencil, a finger moving frenetically across the page as she peered like a myopic sparrow at the guide. 'Can you go out to the kitchen and get my purse?' she said, without looking up.

Susannah hauled herself to her feet, dawdled inside and through to the kitchen. Yawned. Rubbed her eyes. Sleep. Something she vaguely remembered. A sweaty night in tangled sheets searching for a comfy spot on a lumpy mattress, not conducive. The third bedroom was her room. Kept for emergencies. This was where she'd slept after her mother skedaddled to Yass with that other bloke, years ago. The one with the farm and the horses. She was about seven or eight then. Half her life she'd been putting up with Mum's misdemeanors. Could you go through The Change for nine years? That's what Gran reckoned was going on.

She ratted around in the tea-towel drawer for Gran's purse and headed back to the verandah. Finished with the form guide, decision made, Gran prised open the worn, leather purse and extracted two pound notes. She placed them with great care in an envelope and sealed it with a lick. On the outside she'd written: 'Pull the other One, Number Three in the Second at Randwick. A quid each way.' She slapped the envelope on the table in front of Susannah.

'Not wasting money on anything else.' Gran said. She leaned over and absently smoothed Rabbie's ears. 'This gelding's a goer.'

Susannah eyed the envelope. What was the difference between a stayer and a goer? Her job not to reason why, but to head over to Bob's and place the bet. She shoved it into the pocket of her skirt. 'Okay Gran. Will do.'

The sun was higher and there was shade now by way of the old jacaranda that squatted in the middle of the lawn. The garden sloped all the way to the water's edge. At this time of the year the camellias and sasanquas—a bevy of mottled crimson and white, blood red and scorched pink—made a lush scattering of blossoms around the grass. But they short-changed Susannah. For all their gorgeousness, there was no giddy perfume to excite her senses and fertilise her daydreams.

Saturday sailors swarmed on the Harbour. VJs with teenage boys shouting and laughing with the exuberance of life at sea, heavier launches, big yachts unfurling their sails for a day out, motor boats stacked with hopeful fishermen. They all scurried aside for the cream and green ferry churning its way like a stately duchess from Cremorne Point wharf to the Quay.

Thanks to Miss Morrisett, her art teacher at Girls' High, Susannah recognised an early Streeton in wilful, bristling life.

It was all due to Pop. He'd spotted an opening when the market sank just as war broke out and, with the speed of a striking king brown, snaffled up this choice piece of real estate. The house's previous owner, a terrified doctor who was certain the Japs would invade and blow him and his family to Kingdom Come, turned up his nose at selling to a plumber. But he needed the cash so they could bolt for the Blue Mountains and escape the carnage he knew was coming.

'Got it for a bloody song,' Pop always said.

A kookaburra, somewhere close by, set up a mad cackle. Gran caught sight of it in the jacaranda. 'You laughing at us, fella?'

'Yeah,' said Susannah. 'We're a joke. Even the birds think so.'

She toughed it out for the first thirty seconds with a cool saunter. Then, her nerve snapped and she ran for it. She felt the rush of air as the magpie missed his first strike. Bastard! It wasn't nestling season. It was pure malevolence every time she entered his territory. She'd tried everything. A mask worn backwards, topknot hair, sunglasses on the back of her head; nothing fooled him.

Hunched in a coward cringe she arrived at Freddy's Corner Store— 'Best Fish and Chips in Town'. The little bell on the door tinkled as she shuffled in and straightened up. *Who was Freddy?*

Madge had a customer; a bloke chatting her up with a line of patter that—from the sound of it—he figured was irresistible. 'What's a pretty girl like you doing working behind a shop counter?' Susannah winced as the lascivious snigger filtered across to where she idled at the end of the counter next to the big jars. She studied the words on the striped boiled lollies: 'Be my Baby,' and the pretty pink musk hearts inscribed: 'I love you,' 'Dream Girl,' and 'Kiss me'.

The man eventually admitted defeat and headed out. Madge signaled with a nudge of her head, 'Out the back.'

Susannah pushed through the plastic fly strips into Bob's office. The air was thick with stale cigarettes and beery breath. He raised his eyes from a table groaning under the weight of a million scattered slips of paper and eased off his glasses.

'G'day Susannah, 'How ya going? Take a seat.'

'Ta, Bob.' She found a space amid the paper and slipped the envelope on to the table.

He stubbed out his smoke in the overflowing ashtray, exhaling one last perfect blue spiral. He reached a hairy paw and emptied the cash, fixed his glasses on his nose and absorbed Gran's note. He looked mournful. With that sorrowful expression and the jowls bobbling with the shake of his head, Susannah thought he looked like some kind of hound. Except, blood-pressure puce, not brown. He leaned forward on his elbows and a roll from his impressive beer belly bulged against his short-sleeved shirt and settled on the table.

'I'll take her money,' he said. 'But I don't like her choice. Pull The Other One's a bit of a nag. They scratched him last week.'

Susannah shrugged. Did this mean the horse wasn't a goer after all? 'Gran said there was nothing else worth the money.'

Bob scribbled on his pad, tore off the sheet and passed it over.

She put the paper in her pocket. 'I won't tell her you said that. She'll be ropeable if they scratch him.'

Bob gave a short laugh. 'Gamblers' luck.'

Something reckless pulsed through Susannah's veins. She took a deep breath and scrabbled around in her pocket. 'I'll have two bob each way on the same nag, thanks Bob.' She dropped the coins in front of him. *A goer!*

'You serious?' He shook his head in disbelief.

'Gran knows the ponies.'

'Yeah. Has a nose for the long shot, your Gran,' He wrote her a slip for the bet, handed it over and heaved himself to his feet. 'See ya next week.'

She marveled at the thin, hairy legs in their grubby sandshoes sprouting below his work shorts. How could such a skinny pair of pins support Bob's bulk?

The phone booth outside Freddy's always had that smell easing out of its pores. The bad breath and B.O of a thousand users, with an undernote of something visceral that made her eyes water. The pong lingered, no matter what the weather was like. She opened and closed the door a couple of times to clear the air before she shut herself in.

She made a pile of pennies on the shelf. As usual, most of the phone book was missing and the Yellow Pages was only a tattered remnant of its former self. Too bad if you needed to make an urgent call and had to look up the number. Someone had thoughtfully written 'Fuck' in lipstick or blood across the list of emergency numbers on the wall beside the phone.

She inserted the money, dialled, and after three rings pennies clanked into the cash box. From the whispered 'Hello,' she could tell The Man was still in residence.

'Hello Mum. How are you?'

'I'm fine,' came the whisper.

'So. He's still there, then.'

'Yeah. Maybe tomorrow.'

Through the whisper Susannah made out the slurring and the hesitancy. Her mother was well on the way to pissed.

'I've heard that before.'

'I'm really sorry, love. I've asked him to leave. But you know what he's like. Hard to shift.'

She knew that all right. 'Okay. I'll ring tomorrow.'

'I miss you,'

'Yeah. That's likely.' A pause. 'I miss you too.'

'Be a good—'

'Of course. Just like you.' Susannah slammed the receiver back on the hook. No surprises there.

She took a step back into fresh air, breathed in nice and deep and scooted off, contemplating life and her lot in it. Was Mum entitled to a messed-up existence? Was that how it worked? Even if it messed up someone else's? So immersed was she in doleful thinking she neglected the turn of speed required at the border of magpie territory. An ominous rustling in the gum tree on the corner alerted her to imminent danger and she took off.

The nasal whine of the race caller greeted her as, breathless, she made it to safety through Gran's front door. Rabbie snuffled joyfully at her feet and led the way out to the verandah where Gran was tuned to the races.

'Should've backed the mare, turned out a winner, after all,' she muttered, as Susannah handed over the envelope. 'Go and make us a ham sandwich, there's a good girl. Pull The Other One's race is coming up next. He's not the favourite so I stand to win a nice stash if he comes home' Her ear was glued. There was no budging her.

The race was under way by the time Susannah brought out the lunch. Gran was in full flight, making so much noise she could've been in the stand herself. She punched the air and shouted. 'C'mon, you little beauty.' Her eyes lit with the threat of victory. 'He's coming up on the outside!'

Susannah was transfixed. Hands clammy. Heart galloping in time with the horses. She held her breath.

The caller rolled through the names of every horse on the field before returning to the frontrunners. The excitement in his voice almost reached out of the radio to pull them both in. '...and last is Blue Balloon. But coming out of the pack now, on the outside, it's—yes—it's—PULL THE OTHER ONE! He's gonna make it, he's gaining. He's third. He's in second place. And, by golly, winner by a nose is the outsider—'

Whatever else he said was drowned out by Gran's shrieks. 'I knew he was a goer!'

Susannah grinned. 'You can pick 'em, Gran.'

This meant she'd be running another magpie gauntlet to collect the winnings. But what successful punter would ever give a brass razoo about that?

Rumours from a War

Glenn Stuart Beatty

Almost all of the people that I thought of as grown-ups, when I was a child, are dead now, and the last coal mine closed many, many years ago, and is nothing more than a scar on the earth being reclaimed by the stunted ti-tree scrub. I have now earned the right to be called a grown-up, after sixty years in this same town, where I have pre-paid a place in the cemetery.

More than fifty years ago, Autumn mornings came with a layer of fog hanging over the low parts of town, and from every house, from the chimneys of the timber cottages that spread over the hollow to the north of the pit that was now closed down, white smoke emerged that smelled of sulphur. To the little boy, that I once was, the sulphurous smell was of home, and as welcoming as the smell of kittens or freshly baked scones.

It was a Saturday and our Dad had been having a sleep-in after a week of work at the newer pit, the one that sat in the bush a few miles south of the closed one. After he rose from his bed, our Dad liked to sit in his chair in front of the stove with his feet warming on the little shelf below the oven door, where the old tabby cat liked to sleep at night. Our Dad liked to read the paper that I would fetch for him from the front lawn where it had been delivered just before dawn by Mr Knight in his Mini Moke. Our Mum grumbled that our Dad was in the way as she tried to cook the porridge from the oats that she had soaked the night before, but she was probably in a grumpy mood anyway, because, sometime in the next hour, our Dad would make some comment about the porridge not being as good as the porridge his own late mother, who had been born in Stirling, and knew something about porridge, would have made.

Our Dad had a family outing planned for that Saturday which entailed piling into the Holden Special and driving over the mountain range to the lake for some fishing from a jetty, followed by greasy fish and chips and a bottle of beer for our Dad and then a milkshake from the Oak on the way home. My big sister, Annis, decided that she wasn't coming. She was seven years older than me and was having a baby soon. Fred, my brother in law, and Annis had been married for a couple of months, but he had to go to the war in the north with the rest of his mates that our Dad called 'poor bloody nashos.'

It was a good day, even if we didn't catch any fish, until the three o'clock news came on the car radio. Our Dad told me to be quiet when the news came on because he liked to hear what was happening in the world and he was particularly interested in any news from the war in the north. That afternoon, the newsreader told us that there had been a big battle the night before and there had been several soldiers killed and that one of the soldiers was a local boy and that his name was Private Gerald Williams of the Seventh Battalion and that Private Williams came from our town and our Mum burst into tears and our Dad swore which was something he never did in front of our Mum.

I knew Gerald was Fred's mate from the army, and he had introduced Fred to our Annis the Spring before. Fred and Gerald were in the same battalion and did their training together. It had only seemed like a couple of weeks had gone since our Dad had driven Gerald and Fred to the big army base outside of Sydney and I came to keep our Dad company on the drive back home. Gerald said they would be catching a ship to a place called Vung Tau and Fred said it sounded like a stupid name for a place.

Clarrie was an old man who lived next door to us who would give our Mum eggs from his chooks and milk from his goat and our Mum said that he was a widower. One day, just after Fred had left for the war, Clarrie showed me an old yellowed map from one of the National Geographic magazines that he collected and the map was of a place called Indochine and Clarrie pointed out a place on the map that was on the coast and was called Cap Saint-Jacques and he told me that it was an old French name and that Fred would get off the ship there and then go to a place called Nui Dat that wasn't on the old map.

Our Mum was worried that Annis would have heard the same news on the radio that we had, but our Dad said that she never listened to the news and that she didn't watch television, just play records in her bedroom, so she probably hadn't heard about Gerald yet.

When we got home, our Mum went and spoke to Annis in her room. I played with my dog, Zorro in the backyard, throwing balls for him to fetch until our Mum called me in for tea. Annis didn't come and have her tea but stayed in her room. I supposed she might have been crying.

While our Mum was doing the dishes, there was a voice from the back door and it was our neighbour from across the road, Mrs Llewellyn. Where we lived, when people visited, they went to the back door. The front door was only used by official people and a knock on the front door meant bad news like somebody being hurt or killed in the pit. Our Mum told Mrs Llewellyn to come in and asked her if she wanted a cup of tea which Mrs Llewellyn said, 'no thank you' and I could tell that Mrs Llewellyn had something on her mind.

Mrs Llewellyn told our Mum and Dad that Mrs Griffith, who lived next door to Mrs Llewellyn had been spreading rumours that Mrs Llewellyn didn't believe were true. Our Mum used to say that Mrs Griffith was a 'nasty piece of work' who was known to spray children with her garden hose if they played on the footpath outside her house and there was a rumour that she poisoned any cats or dogs that strayed into her yard. The kids who went to big school called her 'Maggie the Baiter'. Maggie's husband was also a nasty man who was a watchman at the closed pit, and he told the local kids that he was a policeman and would send them to the Boy's Home if they played up. Our Dad said Mr Griffith was a scab and our Dad wouldn't even say hello to him in the street.

Mrs Llewellyn said that Maggie the Baiter, although she called her Mrs Griffiths, had told people that while we were out that afternoon that we had some visitors call in and they came in an army car and they were two offices and a minister. Our Mum went white as a ghost and our Dad shook his head and said it was 'a load of rot'. People only got a visit from army officers and a minister if someone had been killed in the war, but the wireless had only mentioned Gerald.

Our Dad went and asked Annis if there had been any visitors while we were out and she said there hadn't and she had been at home all day and when our Dad told her what Maggie the Baiter had been saying, our Annis became a little hysterical and our Dad told her to calm down and that he would ring the army and find out.

Our Dad went into the kitchen and grabbed a handful of five and ten cent pieces from the bowl on top of the fridge where he and our Mum put loose change that they would dole out to me from time to time to buy treats at Mrs Long's corner shop that was at the end of our street. There was a payphone in a bright red box with windows outside of Mrs Long's shop and that was where our Dad would be going to make his call to the army.

I went out the back door to play with Zorro and realised that he wasn't around, and I was scared that he might have wandered off and picked up a bait from Mag Griffith. I walked down the driveway and stood on the footpath and was happy that I could see Zorro standing outside the phone box wagging his tail. He must have followed our Dad when he went to telephone the army and find out what he could about Fred. I decided to walk down the street and keep our Dad and Zorro company.

Eventually our Dad came out of the phone box and said he had spoken to some Major in Victoria Barracks and that the Major said that as far as he was aware, Fred was not on any casualty list and that the army had certainly not sent anyone around to our house. Our Dad seemed very happy and relieved with the news and ruffled my hair as we walked up the street to tell our Mum and Annis that Maggie had been telling lies. Our Mum wondered what it was that would cause Maggie to tell such horrible lies and our Dad said that she was just born nasty and probably couldn't help it and the war brought out the worst in people sometimes and that she must been filled with so much hurt that she wanted to inflict it on others. Our Dad said he heard that Mr Griffiths used to take to Maggie with his fists sometimes,

Two weeks later the whole town turned out for Gerald's funeral including us kids from the school and our Mum made me wear an ironed shirt and we were given little flags on a stick by the teachers and told to form a guard of honour on the street when the hearse went by. My Pa said it was outrageous to make little kids do that and our Dad said that Pa was a communist.

A few weeks after Gerald's funeral, Annis received a large cardboard box in the post and it had lots of stamps on it and she said that it had come from Vung Tau and when she opened it up, it was a reel to reel tape recorder and there were some tapes in boxes and a note from Fred to say that they could send each other tapes instead of letters.

Fred came home a few months later and he went and visited Gerald's Mum but he never talked about what happened the night that Gerald died and when our Dad asked him once, he just shook his head and got a bit teary and said that he thought they were all going to die.

Nobody in the street forgave Maggie the Baiter and all the neighbours refused to talk to her and would turn their backs on her in the shops. Some of the men from the pit would spit at Mr Griffith's feet if they saw him up the shops and they would call him a scab. When he died of a heart attack in his front garden, Maggie screamed for help, but nobody came to see what was happening, but watched from behind their curtains as the ambulance took him away. He didn't have a funeral, just a private cremation Mum said, and Dad said nobody would have turned up anyway. Maggie moved away after that and there were no more rumours in our street.

Save Us, John

Krista Mullally

The Harrington farmhouse was well-known to the community, it was a quaint wooden structure on the side of a hill, home to a couple with a one-year-old girl.

One winter morning, Maura Harrington sat with baby Eva in their living room. Maura rocked her daughter in her arms and tapped her button nose with the tip of her finger. Eva's mouth stretched into a wet smile.

Rather abruptly, the television demanded Maura's attention. She glanced over to the screen and listened to the reporter speak of a predicted storm in their area. Maura craned her neck to face her husband, John, who stood in the kitchen over a sizzling frypan. The tired flame under the pan was burning his bacon.

'Did you hear that?' called Maura.

John arched a brow.

'There's meant to be a storm tonight. We should lock down the sheep, prepare the house-'

'What channel is it?' asked John, finally looking at the television. 'Oh, they're never right. I wouldn't worry about it.'

'John, it's a severe weather warning.'

'Do you remember the last time we did all that? It took hours and there wasn't even a storm. I'm not wasting my time again, but you're free to if you want.'

A wail escaped Eva's lips.

When the storm struck, the Harringtons were holed up in their home. It began as a light pour before transforming into shrieking gusts of wind and daggers of lightning that pierced the distant ground. The sky grew grey and raindrops came down on the farmhouse as waves of bullets that exploded upon the windowpanes and flooded the gutters.

Maura stood at the back window and surveyed the fields. She wasn't used to this kind of misery.

John trod down the staircase and into the living room.

'I told you,' said Maura.

John contemplated an apology, but not for long.

'The important thing is that we're all safe and the sheep are okay. You locked down the barn, right?'

'Yeah. They must be scared to death.'

Maura bit her nails and gazed up at a gumtree that stood just outside the house. It was one of the few gumtrees on their property. Maura always wondered what would happen to it during a storm. As impressive as it was, its magnificent limbs threatened to come crashing through the windows, skewering them all in a bloody wooden mess.

And then it appeared.

Maura only noticed it when John turned away. Her stomach knotted. In the corner of her eye, far out in the distance amongst the weeds and mud on the horizon and trembling in the winds, was a dog. Some kind of ghastly dog, baring the side of its yellow teeth. Its matted fur was the colour of soot and as it crept closer to the farmhouse Maura realised it wasn't exactly a dog, but a horrible beast. Something sent from hell. It was all skinny limbs and fiery amber eyeballs, and it was the size of a grizzly bear.

Maura wondered whether John had seen the dog when he'd been standing by her and decided to turn his back because it was too much hassle for him. He sat on the couch, blowing at the rim of a cup of coffee.

'John, you need to come to the window.' said Maura in a thin voice.

A sigh from John. 'Why?'

The dog crept onto the back porch, eyes locked on Maura's. It sucked in breaths and examined the back window.

'Just tell me what's wrong, don't make me get up for nothing,' bit John.

Maura stormed toward the couch and pulled John over to the back window. He rolled his gaze upward and met the beady eyes of the beast, then clenched his jaw.

'I'll call animal control,' said Maura as she rushed over to the coffee table, grabbing her phone.

'Animal control? You think they're coming out in this weather for a dog?'

Maura looked at her husband as though he were mad. Men could be idiots sometimes.

'It's not just a dog, look at it!'

'All we need to do is kill it. It's just another farm pest, like a 'roo or something. We need to get it between the eyes is all.' barked John.

Maura waited patiently with her phone pressed to her ear but all she heard was a dial tone.

'Oh sure, you just go on outside and grab your shotgun from the shed. You can outrun a dog, right?' she said.

The hound drew a step backward and let out a piercing howl. It was a gut-wrenching noise, a raw screech paired with flying slobber, and John had no clue what it meant. Whatever it was, it set off Eva like an alarm, and she began sobbing at the top of her lungs. Maura hurried upstairs to her.

John didn't like to admit when he was wrong. Or incapable. Or scared. He was sure he could have outrun that dog to get to the shed if he wanted to, but he couldn't push down the fear that lived in his gut, that instinct to stay where it was comfortable and easy.

Another blow of thunder shook the house. Maura rushed downstairs with Eva in her arms as John drew the curtains across the back window. The mutt still whined and snarled from behind the curtains as if it was pushing out its last breaths.

'Ignore that,' said John, 'It still can't get into the house, unless it picks the locks and grows opposable thumbs and turns the doorknob.'

Though she'd never admit it, Maura knew John was right. She held Eva to her chest, laid down on the couch in the living room, wrapped them both up in a blanket, and closed her eyes. It only took a moment for the couple to notice that the back porch had become eerily silent.

'John? Please tell me it's gone.' whispered Maura.

John cautiously walked to the back window and pulled away a corner of the curtain. Puddles and nuts and twigs coated the back porch, but the hound was nowhere to be seen.

Maura's eyes flashed open. She had slept on the couch with Eva, but some noise had ripped her from her slumber, something distorted and high-pitched and pained. She immediately looked down toward her daughter, who was thankfully fast asleep. Maura's heart thrummed in her chest as she approached the window, fingers poised to brush aside the curtains. When she did, she muffled her scream with the palm of her hand.

The porch lights cut through the inky darkness and illuminated the sea of sheep bodies scattered across the grass. Dirty intestines, bowels, viscera strewn by devil teeth across wet grass and mud, pieces laying in an enormous crimson pool. Slinking amongst the magnificent display of organs and waste was the mutt, which wore a demonic grin that split its face in two between the ears. The barn door had been torn open, cast aside on the lawn like debris from a car wreck.

Maura rushed to their bathroom, grasped the sides of their sink, and threw up her dinner.

Maura and John stood at the back window. Maura cradled Eva and John brandished a butcher's knife with a trembling hand. Outside, the dog was pawing at the windowpane and snarling. The glass was thick, but Maura still felt fear churning in the pit of her stomach. She had a sinking feeling that John would panic too much to be able to stand by her. It was a lonely feeling.

'Why don't we drive-'

'Truck's in the shop,' said Maura.

'We could call-'

'Lines are down.'

Then the glass started to crack. A chip appeared, then slowly started to web out as the mutt's claws smashed against it…

John turned on his heel and broke into a run.

'John!' screamed Maura, a lump rising in her throat.

Whilst she watched John's figure disappear through the front doorframe and out onto the road, a bar of lightning struck one of the gumtrees outside, igniting a flurry of orange flames that licked the air. Maura's gaze whipped back to the road outside just in time to see her husband running west. Her face flushed white from fear and humiliation.

Eva erupted into tears.

The dog pawed faster, hungrier.

'John, you son of a-'

Suddenly, the cracks in the window destroyed the glass completely, sending shards of glass raining down upon and sliding across the Harringtons' living room floor. The dog frothed at the newly formed gap in the side of the house, its figure framed by flickering flames in the distance. The house suddenly felt empty and very cold. Maura tightened her grip on Eva and wondered how her home had become so helpless so quickly, and why her wedding band was turning her finger white.

Gales of wind whistled in and out of the farmhouse. The dog stood at the edge of the porch, blinking glass out of its eyes. Maura took the opportunity to race upstairs, gritting her teeth as debris cut up the bottom of her feet. She held Eva close to her chest as she flew up the staircase and into the nursery, tucking them both away in the corner between a rocking chair and a toy box. The door's lock clicked behind her. Maura sucked in breaths and pretended she couldn't hear the ravenous mutt tearing its way through the house, a tornado with an empty stomach. Breaking lamps, upturning tables, trampling photo albums.

'I'm your mother. I won't let it take you.' Maura looked down at Eva.

A large body beat, beat, beat against the nursery door. The door's hinges shuddered and cried out and the piece of wood would ultimately give way, it was only a matter of seconds. Maura pressed her cheek against her infant's head and peered out the nursery window toward the dead grass and the sheep carcasses, and she tried to contain the heaving sobs that swelled within her chest. The weather would steal her home from her and so would this dog. Hey eyes started to water.

The door burst open with a bang and standing in the open doorway, growling through its teeth, was the beast. It was an enormous figure of smoke and death. It quickly thundered into the room and turned its jaws to the child first, the small pillow of flesh that would go down its throat like warm butter, but within seconds she had slipped out of sight. Maura had slid Eva across the floor and toward the open doorway.

'Run, Eva, please!' choked Maura.

And Eva, upon seeing her mother lunge at the dog, started to cry. Maura and the dog were a tangle of fur and skin and blood and limbs, there were screams and snarls and, very quickly, an earsplitting crack as Maura's neck snapped under the strength of the dog's jaws. Eva began crawling away as the hound feasted on her mother's spilled organs, but she didn't make it past the top stair before the dog turned to face her.

The dog trotted down the staircase and through the wreckage of the living room. All sorts of wreckage were scattered across the living room floor: leaves and photo frames and wooden pieces, bathed in the darkness flooding in from the east side of the house. The house that had served as the Harringtons' sanctuary for so many years had been slaughtered and reeked of heartbreak.

The dog's ribcage bulged against the remaining flesh of its belly as it picked its way to the open doorway and walked out onto the open road. The Australian countryside always looked very empty, but it had never been as barren as it was after the storm. The hound raised its nose, grunting and smelling the air, before leaving behind the ruins of the farmhouse and heading west.

The Coffin

Carol Middleton

The coffin would only need to be small but to be authentic, it would have to have six sides. That would be harder to make than a box with four sides. The image of a coffin was clear in her mind's eye: two short sides, two long sides and two end pieces. He, the mathematical one, drew a hexagon on a sheet of paper and did some calculations.

The workshop was set aside from the farmhouse that belonged to their architect friend. For the moment it was a refuge from the pity in the house. The sawdust and silence helped deaden the pain. The architect showed them the tools to use.

'I can make it for you. It's easy for me. Let me do it.'

But it was their job. They needed to do this. He marked out the sheets of pine and she helped him cut them out with the bandsaw. The architect hovered as they contemplated how to join the pieces. The joints had to be strong enough to take the weight and keep the box together as it was lowered into the grave.

The previous day they had visited the village undertaker, who assessed the situation. Like most of his customers, these people were ignorant and uninformed. And, like the rest, they would not have any choice in the matter. The undertaker delved into an ancient filing cabinet and retrieved the relevant documents. He offered them a funeral package that included a miniature coffin lined with swan's-down. He slid the price list across the smooth surface of the mahogany desk. They stared at the long numbers and the cherubs blowing trumpets in the margins, then walked out of the airless office into the bright spring day. Their mind was made up.

No one could tell them if it was legal. They knew you couldn't bury the dead in unconsecrated ground. So digging a grave under the oak tree at the farm was out of the question. There was an old church on top of the hill with a graveyard overlooking the valley. That would be fine. Normally, the undertaker took the body from the morgue to the funeral parlour and then to the grave. Could they cut him and his hearse and his swan's-down coffin out of the proceedings and take a homemade coffin to the churchyard themselves in their old Morris Traveller?

They drove to the council chambers and persuaded an official to look up the regulations. Confronted by the couple with their worn clothes and long hair, the man was scathing but, intrigued by the novelty of the request, pulled down several volumes of byelaws from the shelves. He was surprised to discover the law was in the young people's favour. He turned the closely printed book around on the counter, so they could read the verdict for themselves. There was no mention of undertakers or third parties in the legal description of burying the dead.

They parked the Morris in the hospital car park and took the box out of the back. Every passer-by turned to stare. No doubt it was the shape of the box. And the size. And the young man who carried it under his arm. And the young woman beside him. The onlookers stood still, until the spectacle disappeared down the ramp.

The morgue was in the basement of the hospital complex. The cold air hit them as they pushed open the glass doors and walked up to the desk, where they set down the raw wood coffin. The attendant had been told to expect a couple acting on their own behalf, and registered no surprise. He scrutinised the official form they had prepared and took out a set of keys. He walked down the second row of metal cabinets and unlocked one of the large drawers. He checked the tag on the contents, took out a small plastic bundle, returned to the desk and placed the package in the coffin.

'Sign here.'

The young man lifted the box, now a few pounds heavier. He hoisted it on to his shoulder and turned to go, avoiding the gaze of the discreet official. She closed the glass doors behind them, preparing herself for more stares of disbelief in the car park. But it was deserted. There were no witnesses, no judge and no jury. Just them, the three of them, and that was all that mattered. They had made their decision and now they would do whatever else there was left to do.

When they arrived home, he left her alone.

She waited, frightened of unwrapping the bundle, but finally took a pair of scissors and cut a neat slit in the white plastic. The baby was clothed. She was wearing a white paper dress and bonnet. Some other woman must have done this for her. Her face was the same: peachy skin with high cheekbones and her lips still pink. The mother touched the face, but it did not give. It was rock hard, frozen. The eyes would not open. She kissed it, but it did not move.

She lined the coffin with an off-cut of soft cotton, laid the child in this nest and carried it outside. She opened the back doors of the old Morris and set the coffin on display inside. The car was parked in front of the farmhouse, next to the driveway, where everyone left their cars, so friends would be able to admire her daughter when they arrived for the funeral.

He made tea. One of the women, a young mother, gave her a crystal for the baby to hold. Some brought daffodils and crocuses. They embraced the woman briefly, not sure if she would collapse in their arms. They didn't say much. No one looked in the coffin. Her baby lay out there alone and ignored. *Look at her. She is perfect. You must look. I think of nothing but her face and the bliss of giving birth to her. When she lay on my lap, I was a woman at last. I am not that woman now. I am still here for her, but she no longer needs me. Look at her. Please look at her.*

In the evening she put the lid on the coffin and shut the back doors of the Morris. The mother and father drove up the hillside in their best clothes. The vicar met them at the churchyard and they carried the coffin to the grave. There was a deep hole, and a man leaning on a shovel. Ropes straddled the hole. They set the box on the ground and held hands. The vicar was kind and the words he spoke were respectful. She watched the trees move in a hilltop breeze. It was a good spot.

The men in the party took hold of the ropes and balanced the little box on them.

'Slowly,' said the father, but the coffin rolled off the ropes just before it hit the hard clay at the bottom of the grave. There was a thud. She pictured the crystal rolling out of the child's folded hands. The mother and father exchanged a wry smile. They threw hedgerow flowers into the hole before the earth was shovelled back.

The milk surged in her engorged breasts and leaked through her white dress.

I should have taken you in my arms straight away. When I held you, the heat flooded me. I would have kept you warm and held the life in you, but they took you away, wrapped you in cloths and pads.

He put his arm around her.

'We'll have to make a cross to mark the grave. We'll be back.'

They never did go back. Within a week they had packed up and moved on. They contrived some destination and followed the road. But somewhere on a Welsh hilltop, there still remain the vestiges of their child.

The Koel

Susan McCreery

For a long time Beverly had struggled with what to write on the *Happy Birthday, Son* card for Jimmy's sixtieth just gone. In the end, she decided on something neutral and straightforward – *With best wishes from your mother* – hoping Caroline would decide against flipping the card into the bin.

It was the call of a koel that had woken her, the only sound in the dead-of-night neighbourhood. Up, up, UP it went. Beverly lay in bed, her thoughts flitting back and forth between Jimmy's birthday, and fledglings and occupied nests. She wondered if there'd been a party. She knew not to expect an invitation. Her relationship with Caroline had never recovered after the wedding, when in a tipsy misery of regret Beverly had sashayed across the floor to prise Jimmy out of his bride's arms. Visits – and eventually even Jimmy's solo drop-ins – dropped off. He was busy with the baby. Caroline needed him at home. He was *snowed under.*

Up, up, UP went the koel. With no hope of sleeping, Beverly eased her legs out from under the covers and moved unsteadily to the window, where she twisted the venetians until she could see the house next door. She pictured three-year-old Erin in her little bed. The new baby in a milk-fed slumber in its Moses basket. Then her thoughts turned to the father, Paolo. Would his eyes flip open at the sound of the baby's first dawn cry? It wasn't so long ago that Beverly had snuck over there to peer in the bedroom window as he slept, Felicity a big pregnant mound beside him. Paolo, she'd concluded, must have been watching her through his lashes. Nothing was ever said, but Beverly had noticed Erin no longer dragged her little toilet stool across the yard to say 'Hello, lady' over the fence.

The loose palings remained unnoticed, hidden under the potato vine. An invitation and a secret.

Beverly didn't own a microwave, didn't want one. She was attuned to the precise moment you took the saucepan off the stove, seconds before the milk rose in a sudden upwelling of white froth. If she ever, as a new mother, mistimed it, Jimmy would jerk his head back in shock and pain, his pink tunnel of a screaming mouth strung with milky threads.

The koel had gone quiet. Beverly lifted the saucepan and poured the milk into a mug, adding two spoonfuls of Ovaltine. She'd breastfed for as long as she could stand it. It wasn't easy, those early days. She thought of Felicity next door, bringing the baby out to the Sunday luncheon table, then undoing her maternity bra (in full view of all the guests!), pushing the little one's head onto her breast, all the while shiny-laughing as though she was surrounded by everything she'd ever wanted, as though her life was complete. Beverly had never known such a Sunday. Had never relaxed at the table as her husband laid out great platters of Mediterranean food, dropping a kiss on her head as he passed.

Often, on weekday afternoons, the delicious aroma of Paolo's cooking – garlic, spices, herbs – would waft through her windows. After a while, Beverly would see him emerge, the new baby cocooned at his chest, his big forearms flexing as he unfolded the stroller for Erin. Out they'd go, not returning for at least an hour, leaving Felicity, Beverly assumed, luxuriating in some free time.

She'd had no such free time, no such husband.

When Beverly's father had forbidden the relationship (*Not having any of that wog filth in here. Catholic muck.*), Antonio had made plans for them to flee interstate. He'd find work in the Queensland cane fields, he told Beverly. *You'll be of age soon. No one can stop us.* And then it had all stopped, like a horse pulling up at a tangle of barbed wire. Beverly had never heard from Antonio again. She recalled the heat of his chest, his arms that shone with an olive lustre. Arms that pulled her to him, pressed her head to his heart.

She'd married Bruce from church. Mottle-skinned Bruce.

Bruce had turned out to be Not Very Nice.

Was it worth the effort to go back to bed? By the time she'd climbed the stairs, shucked off her slippers, and waited for sleep to overtake her, the sun would be up. Monday was Paolo's day to work at the city office. Felicity would take Erin and the baby out at about ten. Beverly pictured all the young mums sitting on picnic rugs with takeaway coffees. There would be a slice, or a cake, and some silly ready-mades for the toddlers to eat, like Tiny Teddies or TeeVee Snacks. Such things were unheard of in the sixties. Beverley stretched out on the couch, pulling the rug over her.

When she woke, her mouth was dry and the sun was harsh and bright. For her entire life she'd been an early riser. But this was the third sleep-in, and the longest, in the last couple of weeks.

Felicity was dressed in a sleeveless, belted pinafore, in a pale yellow and pink, buttoned down the front. It hadn't rained in weeks, so Erin's shiny red gumboots were quite unnecessary – the sign of an over-indulgent mother, thought Beverly. Whenever Jimmy had appeared in his cowboy outfit to attend church or some other function, he was given a slap and an instruction to about-face and change into his checked shirt and khaki cub-Scout shorts.

As Felicity was strapping Erin into the stroller (laden with bags), Beverly caught sight of an inky mark on the young mother's back. She lifted her binoculars. 'Oh, lord,' she muttered, screwing up her nose. Tiny bluebird or not, it was still a tattoo. She pinched the skin on her arm. Felicity had no notion what forty or fifty years would do to the bird, how it would end up distorted in a speckled corduroy of flesh.

Antonio had married one of his own, Beverly later learned. Quite the beauty. They'd had a baby seven months after the wedding, which meant all that time Antonio had been pressing Beverly to his heart he'd also been pressing himself between the beauty's legs. They brought forth another baby the following year. Beverly would catch a bus, saying she was shopping for cloth at Silverwater, but instead, wearing a headscarf and dark glasses, she would wheel Jimmy past their house, until one day it was closed and shuttered, a For Rent sign stuck in the tall, seedy grass.

Beverly should have seized Antonio, pulled him between her own legs, made it impossible for him to leave her. The heat that had pulsed within her when she was young! What power it held. She would have grasped his hand and *flown* with him to Central station, *laughing*.

Beverly looked down to see that her fingers still held her skin in a pincer. A bruise would likely form. There was also a ginger cat twining in and out of her legs, making short yowling noises. Someone should feed it.

In the kitchen was a frightening jumble of unwashed Willow Patterns, knives and forks at careless angles, a hardened smear of yellow egg on the topmost plate. How could this be? Whatever their evenings had held – silent disregard, fury or cold congress – the cast-iron rule was always dishes before bed.

The sound of the postie scooter brought Beverly back to the present. She was still in her nightie, she noticed, but what did it matter? Apart from slipping through the fence, she had no plans for the day. None, at least, that required a change of clothes. When she opened the pantry, she felt as startled as Alice in Wonderland, confronted by cat faces grinning at her from a stack of small cans. She took a purple one and used her fingers to scoop the lot onto a saucer. She placed the empty tin on the eggy plate. Licked her fingers clean.

Beverly ducked under the potato vine. A ripping sound told of another hole in her nightie, and what was the difference?

Among the spinach and lettuce in the vegie patch was Italian parsley and a neat row of new chilli plants. So very Mediterranean! Beverly made her way cautiously round the side of the house until she came to the bedroom window. Behind the bed hung a huge portrait of the young couple grinning in a soft shaft of sunshine on a winding path at the base of a rocky hill. There was even an ancient olive tree, and a goat. Paolo could be a David Jones catalogue model, Beverly thought. She peered through the window at the rumpled bed, the ice-white linen sheets, his boxer shorts on the pillow. On the floor lay his beloved tan boat shoes, scuffed and faded.

Beverly glanced about her, her heart clip-clopping, and continued on to follow the perimeter of the house until she arrived at the front door. She placed her hand on the doorknob, but whisked it away as the postie puttered to a stop to slip an envelope into the letterbox. Beverly gave him a hearty wave, and when he'd gone she brought out the eggy plate and the empty cat food tin concealed behind her back.

Leaning forward, she placed them both on the doormat then brushed her hands together with satisfaction, saying, 'That's that, then.'

Crossing the backyard again, Beverly paused by the vegie bed to reach down and uproot the row of chillis, then fling them onto the back step. She imagined Felicity looking puzzled and saying to Paolo, 'Do you think it was a cockatoo?'

Was it night or day? Time had warped. Day, of course, *of course*, thought Beverly. Time for a nana nap for a nana who was not. Once again, she lay down on the couch, pulling the rug over her.

The cat had something in its jaw. It kept dropping it, readjusting its grip, picking it up again. Specks of blood on the kitchen floor. A mother cat with its wounded kitten. Mewling. Mewling so loudly it woke Beverly, and through the blur of consciousness she came to understand it was no kitten but a human baby. Felicity and the children must be home. And whose cat was this, sprawled, rumbling, across her chest? Beverly fell down the well of sleep once more, not waking until it was dark.

Had she eaten? She recalled scooping meat out of a tin. The soles of her feet were tacky. Whose face was that, reflected in the side of the toaster? Whose nightie? She pulled the empty knife across a surface of charcoal.

The squeal of a child: 'Look, the stars! Look, the moon!'

'Come and brush your teeth.'

Who was singing?

'Antonio, is that you?' cried Beverly, wiping the toast crumbs from her lips.

She should dress for the night. Something captivating. Something dark with feathers.

No lights.

All the better to see them by.

She would not sleep tonight. She would climb to her perch, and from on high she would call, 'Look up, up, UP.'

There is

Alan Whelan

Eliza Tregarthen, widow, opened the door of her house in Cook's Hill, Newcastle, half swamp and half coalminers' shacks. The late Jonas, a clergyman who'd made more money than an honest man, had bought one of the district's respectable houses. She looked out at the Corlette Street Park and frowned. She'd expected a hawker or a beggar at the door; there'd been more since the Illawarra colliery strike. Then she looked down.

A child awaited her attention, in a red coat tricked out with bands and curlicues of gold braid, tight white pantaloons and a white wig. He looked like a pageboy in a Mozart opera, or *Der Rosenkavalier*.

Eliza was not yet twenty-eight, with her waist held to nineteen inches in whalebone and crinoline. She was out of mourning for Jonas, so her hair was unveiled, long, fair and straight. She said, 'What would you like, young man?'

The boy tried to look stern. 'My master said I shouldn't talk.' Then he realised he *had* and closed his mouth abruptly. He stood silent, looking down, but lifted his arms to hold out an envelope and a parcel.

She accepted them, astonished. Then she remembered that the boy might look extraordinary but he *was* a boy, short for his perhaps nine years. 'Can I get you something? I believe Cook has left toffee in the kitchen.'

The boy kept his lips almost closed so he wasn't breaking his master's order too gravely. 'I'm not supposed to accept anything from you.' He drew himself up to his full height, only a short way above her waist. Then he wheeled about and was gone.

She opened the parcel first: strawberries. So she opened the envelope, expecting to find a handwritten poem, the kind that threatens to compare to the enclosed fruit her nipples – about which the author could know nothing – and her lips.

Instead the envelope contained a plain tan card more suited to business than to *billets-doux*, and it featured only two words, in Gothic lettering: 'There is.'

Eliza turned it over. The card said nothing else, and neither it nor the envelope gave any clue concerning the sender. She sniffed it. It was not scented. She shrugged, and absent-mindedly took a strawberry.

The next day the boy was back. He was silent this time, and none of her wiles could get him to spill a word. When he'd left she opened the package. It contained Turkish delight. She set it aside. This card was slightly wordier. It said, 'A man who,' ending with a comma.

Eliza frowned. Women in Newcastle society had tried to bring her to social events once she'd broken her mourning, but so far she'd refused them. Interest from a man was unexpected. She supposed it must be someone nearby, though she knew no one in Corlette or Parry Street likely to employ this boy or clothe him in such an extraordinary way. She put the card in her writing desk.

The next day's card read, 'Enamoured of your wit and grace' and was accompanied by pomegranates. An educated man, then, if not a poet. She knew from Jonas, who had studied Hebrew, that the pomegranates referred to the garden between her thighs, which the King James version of *The Song of Songs which is Solomon's* euphemistically called her 'branches'.

The next day the boy delivered chocolate, and the card read: 'And the loveliness of your face.'

She had a suitor with a dramatic sense. She knew that she was pleased: she had never been a simpering miss, or a hypocrite. Whoever he was, he was having fun, and she was enjoying his campaign.

There were thirteen deliveries, with sweets, marzipan and little sweet cakes, and a small flask of an Italian liqueur that smelled of truffles. Together, the texts read: 'There is / A man who, / Enamoured of your wit and grace / And the loveliness of your face, / Abandons all thoughts of duty / Fallen faint before your beauty. / The sweetest thing that I could do / Would be to spend my time with you. / Enchanting Lady, / I seek an hour / In your sweetest company / If I came to your bower / Tomorrow at nine, please excuse and admit me.'

The last card, with its abominable scansion, was accompanied by the liqueur. The boy had taken to paying awkward compliments of his own: he called her 'beautiful ma'am'. She'd realised that he was actually over twelve and, though not a dwarf, he would never be tall. He had the ardour of the young man he nearly was.

Her suitor called at nine in the evening. The time, when the neighbours most interested in the doings of their neighbours had closed their curtains and retired, betrayed his intentions, but his gifts and cards had made that plain anyway. He was tall and well dressed in a simple dark suit, with broad shoulders and a fierce moustache. He said his name was Thomas.

There was laughter in his eyes as she admitted him, and she found him very pleasant company. By ten she was on her sofa talking about her family, and speaking of the late Jonas, cleric and rogue, and Thomas was sitting opposite her in a chair he'd placed for the purpose, rubbing her feet. By eleven they had kissed. By midnight she had permitted a man to see her undress, and he had joined her, naked, in bed.

She hoped that Mrs Parsloe next door, whose hearing was unhelpfully keen, would interpret any sounds she heard as the yowling of Corlette Street cats. He let himself out at four, before the first glimmer of dawn or the stirring of the earliest tradesman or labourer.

She was surprised not to hear from him again, but two days later she saw the pageboy leave the Parry Street house where lived Bridget O'Faolain, whose husband had died in the Stockton Colliery fall. The next day she waylaid the boy, seizing the card. It said, 'Fallen faint before your beauty': that meant, she calculated, that the campaign for Brigit was on its seventh day, and it had been launched before Thomas had spent the night with her.

She clutched the boy's collar. 'You know these messages are the same he sent me? I'll bet that package is full of brandy balls.' She spoke bitterly. 'Those arrive on the sixth day, do they not? And you, I thought you were a charming young man, a Cherubino. But you are only Leporello, depraved and cruel.'

The boy stared at her. In Mozart's opera, Leporello is the cynical procurer for his heartless master, Don Giovanni. 'But Leporello is condemned to hell, beautiful ma'am. I swear I don't know what these packages and cards say. Why are they heartless?' He hated that she was angry with him; he was near tears.

So Eliza explained some things about men and women, and how unmarried women were expected to behave in Newcastle in the year of our Lord 1896, and the damage to their hearts and their social standing that his master was uncaringly risking. She let her anger, which included all Newcastle as well as Thomas, free. The boy listened to her, visibly appalled, and eventually Eliza relented and took his hand. 'I'm sure you were innocent, boy.'

'Eustace.'

'Eustace, for you there's nothing to forgive. Your master is unforgivable.'

'He is! I did not wish to cause you any hurt, ma'am. You are,' he swallowed, 'gracious. But he has used me to hurt many beautiful women. Fear not, ma'am, he will pay. You shall be avenged.' He was saying something he'd read in a book.

Even so: 'Now, Eustace, let's—'

But he stalked away. Bridget never received her card and brandy balls. Eliza watched him walk down Parry Street, then followed him into Bruce Street. She saw him enter a terraced house across the road from the Cricket Ground.

She returned to that house the next day to confront Thomas. A pretty woman, a year or two younger than Eliza, was leaving, quickly, head down. Eliza knocked on the door, but it swung open. The woman hadn't closed it properly. She stepped inside. She made her voice stern, though a faint tendril of fear touched her heart: 'Thomas!'

She found him in his dark wood parlour, collapsed against a wall. There was a kitchen knife, a meat knife, protruding from his shirt and, the dark stain confirmed, from him. He bled, too, from a cut on his face. His eyes were closed, but he breathed. Eustace was on his knees, dabbing ineffectually at the blood flowing from his face. Eliza tightened her lips and stepped forward. 'Eustace!'

'This is my fault, Ma'am!'

'Lower him to the floor, properly, so he's flat. And stand away.' The knife wasn't in the right place, at the right angle, to have pierced any mortal organ. She knelt beside Thomas, grasped the knife and pulled it out. Blood gushed but did not spurt. Thomas jerked in pain, groaned and opened his eyes.

She pulled off his jacket and tore away his shirt and, when Eustace returned with a sheet cut into strips, bandaged him as tightly as she could. Eustace watched, weeping, 'I told all the women what my master was doing. One came and… I never expected it to be so…'

Thomas stirred. 'Melodramatic,' he murmured. 'Anyway, Eustace, I cut myself. A kitchen accident. You saw nothing else and you are to say nothing else.'

Eliza said, 'Eustace, fetch a doctor.'

Thomas nodded, and said, 'McKenzie.' Eustace left, quickly.

Eliza frowned. 'A doctor will not believe your story.'

'He will think what he likes. I'll enjoin him to say nothing. I would like the same favour from you.'

Eliza sighed. At last she agreed. He was protecting his attacker, which spoke well of him. And, she conceded, he had used a *capote* during their night together, so there were limits to his irresponsibility. He had been good company and she had missed such company.

'I suppose you will tell me that I got what I deserved.'

'No. I'd prefer that you were a more honest man, but I did not wish to see you dead. Or even wounded. Well, not more than slightly.'

He was pale but he managed to smile. 'That's very kind. I wonder if you would accept a visit from me, when I am recovered?'

'Would you want to see Bridget too? And the woman who stabbed you?'

Thomas grunted. Pain is tiring, she knew. But he said, 'She'd like to know she doesn't have to mourn me. And Bridget is a nice girl.'

That came close to honesty, she thought. 'You take women too lightly. Eustace did right when he told all your women what you were up to.'

'I suppose you could see it that way. I'd like to kick his arse. When I am recovered.'

'Then Eustace needs a new situation. He can work for me. Until he can work for himself.'

Thomas nodded. Then he closed his eyes. 'Eustace will soon return. I suggest you should not be here when McKenzie arrives. If you would keep your good name.'

Blood blossomed through the rough bandage she had made for him. But sheets are not very absorbent and she judged it looked worse than it was. He would not die. Nor would the rules of Newcastle die, under which she must live, or seem to. Eliza stood. 'I would willingly tell Newcastle society how to dispose of my name. And it's odd of you to be thinking about it now. But I will go.'

He said nothing. At the door she turned back. 'Send Eustace to me, for a position.' She thought, angrily, of Newcastle society. And wished its rules to perdition. 'And … yes, if you can be discreet, I may permit you to visit him, in his new home, from time to time.'

Gold

Jenni Mazaraki

The land was cheap.

The house built in eighteen months. Fresh trees planted in the backyard, no higher than their shoulders. *They'll be shade soon enough,* said Mikolaj when Tess pinched her lower lip with the top one. *You'll see.*

In the outer suburbs of Melbourne, the trees were few. Developers had rushed in and flattened the land. Concrete driveways lead to vacant blocks, awaiting new owners. Waiting for their purpose to be fulfilled

Mikolaj had never owned a garden of his own. In the flat he used to share with his parents in Poland, his mother kept several indoor plants that she dusted with a damp sponge, like ornaments. Now, he planted apple trees, pears and peaches. The vegetables grew in the raised garden bed—tomatoes, broad beans, dill. He built a shed in the corner of the backyard, to hold everything he wanted to fix. But the trees did not fruit, the leaves curled and dropped to the ground. He went to the nursery again and again. Dug more holes in the soil.

When finally, the first tomato bloomed red across its glossy surface, Mikolaj plucked it from the plant and offered it to his son like a jewel. The child grinned as he bit into it, juices running down his small chin.

Everything felt solid until that day. The neighbour knocked on the door and handed Tess a letter. *It explains it all,* said the neighbour, *it's arsenic, in the ground. That's why nothing grows.*

After closing the door, Tess walked to the living room and lay down on the carpet, staring up at the freshly painted ceiling. She remembered the Opéra Garnier ceiling in Paris, the Chagall spreading like a natural thing above her as the music played and the dancers danced. Everything had seemed solid in Paris. The museum with the dinosaur bones reassembled. The Louvre, the university, Notre Dame.

She had grown up knowing about abandoned gold mines in the Australian bush, knew to be wary of shafts disguised by years of overgrowth. Cautious of not falling underground with collapsed soil when bushwalking. Knew to stick to the path. She understood how to focus her mind, keep the danger at bay.

Now, the shifting of ground beneath her feet came closer until it was right there in the room with her. All of the fear in the world refused to leave her alone.

Mashed carrots splattered her jeans. She returned to her child in his high chair, heard him calling for more.

Like Tess, Mikolaj had been in Paris for a semester at the university. He made friends quickly, saw the best in people. Their history subject brought a group of students together but spent more time drinking and going to clubs than studying. Sinking into saggy old couches at new friend's houses, talking without pause, the night air wrapping around them. At the end of the month together, he told her, *ja kocham ciebie.* With his hand a perfect fit for her own, she didn't need a translation to understand.

In the furniture shop they sat on chairs worth a small fortune, dropping crumbs from their sweet pastries, before the salesman waved them out like garbage. Walking breathlessly through streets where revolutions had come and gone, kissing in doorways, laughing. Their history studies forgotten, minds and bodies fixed only on the future.

The panini warm, the crust crisp, the cheese soft, enveloping her tongue. Wrapped in paper that made the sound of everything good. Walking around Paris together, each cobblestone beneath their feet, welcoming.

In autumn, the trees held still in the park. Luxembourg Gardens cloaked itself in quiet, the morning mist hovering around leather boots and woollen jackets. Breath drifted around cheeks, eyes focused on the pathways to work. They lingered, sat on a bench under a neatly clipped tree. Hiding its true form in geometry.

Sheltered from the cold sky, Tess noticed a strip of grey between each tree. She huddled closer to Mikolaj in her thin jacket, made for a mild Australian winter, not a European chill. She felt the bench beneath her body, saw the woman sitting opposite, a shaggy brown coat covering her knees. The woman's cigarette smoke silently filling the space between them.

Versailles and its dilapidated halls unnerved her. Couldn't wait to escape its dusty rooms. Filled with echoes of pale aristocrats, faces painted with lead cosmetics. A vanity that killed. The gold leaf, peeling at the edges. The hall of mirrors bounced every part of her across the space. Saw herself trapped and released, a ricochet of all she was in the late afternoon light, her skin warmed by the sun, imperfections illuminated and celebrated in the glass, streaked and battered by the ages. Hers, another face to capture briefly before disappearing forever. The noise from other travellers and the click, clicking of cameras. The well-rehearsed voices of tour guides passing through, not quickly enough. It was too much, the noise.

I met someone, Tess messaged her sister. *He's coming home with me.*

She had longed for trees, wild and untamed. Told Mikolaj about the air scented with eucalypt and filled with the bird sounds she knew. Back in Australia, the drive along the freeway from the airport passed by low buildings sparsely placed, tin sheds of metal and concrete. Coloured blue and orange and white. The hardy plants on the side of the road, neglected and wiry. Nobody's. Required to survive without anything more but the minimum of care. No unnecessarily ornate structures here.

It was as though she noticed the sky for the first time. The expanse did not end at the horizon, the road, or at the row of trees, tinder dry. These days, spring was as hot as summer.

So beautiful, unbelievable, all this space. Mikolaj's eyes took it all in. *Like a dream,* he said.

They were married at the lavender farm. Their wedding bands made from the melted gold of Mikolaj's family heirlooms his mother had given for this purpose. He knew that Tess didn't want a diamond, didn't want blood on her hands. His parents had known days of living without and taught Mikolaj not to be wasteful with things or time or love. Mikolaj's mother had always stocked up on tinned food, made preserves and jams. Always preparing for leaner times.

With Tess's studies finished, she began a job at the museum. Mikolaj had already been working at a nearby engineering firm making bits of metal fit together smoothly.

In his spare time, he couldn't resist fixing things, picking scraps up from the side of the road. Saved from landfill. Resources spared. In his shed, out the back, he learned how to repair broken things. Almost as good as new. He didn't mind scratches or dents, didn't mind an oddly shaped mend. Proud as a schoolboy at the end of a race. Presented his objects to his wife like a prize. His joy was infectious. She caught his beaming face in her own. Sunshine between them.

The baby born without fanfare. An easy birth, slipping from her into the day. Began his life like a fish swimming in his father's arms. *Look at him go,* said Mikolaj with admiration, holding the squirming child gently.

A murmur, they said, *nothing serious, we'll just keep an eye on it.* Their son's tiny heart made an unusual sound, a disruption to the smooth sailing they expected, had hoped for.

Come stay with us until you get the house stuff sorted. Her sister cleared the spare room, *stay as long as you need to.* Mikolaj stood in the doorway before Tess left with the baby. *I'll fix it my love, you'll see.* He reached for her hand. *Don't go.*

She would not risk her baby's health. The house could fall into the earth and never be returned for all she cared.

It was in the news now. People knew her name. The class action was going to be long and drawn out. It would be years before they would see any justice. Even then, she knew there was no such thing. She did not want to be media fodder, chased down the street for comment. She left her house, her garden. Built on a former gold mine. Poisons leaching into the ground, the water pipes, every surface. People up and down the street, sick. Contaminated.

At least it's not the murder house, Tess. Her sister raised her eyebrows and offered a toothy smile. They had spent months together, before the block of land was bought, when Mikolaj couldn't make the inspection times, visiting house after house. Queuing to see walls patched poorly, carpets steam cleaned with stains still evident. They recognised the odour of blood in damp carpet, saw the pond shaped stain in the living room floor between hired furniture. *Just water damage,* said the poker faced real estate agent. At the sight of her sister's grin, Tess shook her head and laughed.

In her sister's house they played cards, sang songs to each other's children, baked biscuits. In between, Tess made phone calls; to lawyers, to people who might help. Each time she put the phone down she felt her body sinking.

The fires had been burning for weeks. Last year, Notre Dame burned down. That stone structure made by man. This year, Australia caught fire and it was burning still. A never-ending destruction. It did not come close to them, never was a question of threat or danger in the suburbs. They could turn off the news and not have the burning here in the room or in their heads. They could go to the shops, to the pool, to the park and not even think of it. Only when the smoke weighed down on the streets, the washing still left on the line, brought inside, reeking, did they pay attention. When the EPA recommended they stay inside, their chests tightened.

Eventually you're going to have to start thinking about something other than fire and arsenic, Tess. Her sister could see Tess falling. *We still have to live.* But Tess could not stop thinking. She held her ear to her son's chest often, waited to hear the rhythm constant and familiar before turning to other tasks.

As children, Tess and her sister played games.

Would you rather be boiling hot or freezing cold? Eat only pizza forever or ice-cream? Live a long, boring life or an exciting, short life?

Should we get face masks? An air purifier?

The smoke had enveloped Melbourne, sat heavy in the valley, kept in by the Dandenong Ranges, without release from wind. The air had been still for days. Tess stocked up like a doomsday prepper. The cupboard was filled with face masks, toilet paper, tinned food, medications.

Mikolaj wrapped his arms around her. *Try not to worry, my love, it will pass.*

Her baby woke at night at the usual time but could not be comforted in his cot with the gentle pat, patting. She lowered the side rail of the cot, lifted the wailing child and pulled him close. Always warmed by that moment when she felt him curl into her. Tucked him into her bed as she had most nights, held him softly and soothed him gently with her voice, her hand stroking his forehead, left to right. He settled, the scent of her soothing his tiny lungs, and slept.

In the early morning, Tess woke slowly from her dream—of her child-self sitting by the edge of a hole, waiting. Something was down there that she could not see, unreachable. Rubbing the sleep from her eyes, thought she could see a haze hovering above the bed. On the bed, her son's body still. No air pushing in and out of his smoke-filled lungs. She put her ear to his chest, fires burning into the sky hundreds of kilometres away, the light from underneath the curtains, entering the quiet room, golden.

The Baby Store

Eleanor Limprecht

'But we have what we came for.'

'Just a minute, love. I want to make sure there's nothing *else.*'

Louisa sat at the register, listening to the couple beside the display of Baby Bandana Drool Bibs. He came out of the aisle, stocky and thick-necked, tatts up his arms to wait beside the register for his wife. Or partner. Louisa never assumed. She gave the man a sympathetic smile and went back to ordering more stripy rompers online. 'How long 'til divorce' was a game the car seat fitters played. They would have fun with these two.

'Cherise is not going to be happy until she's bought the bloody store,' the bloke said.

Cherise's voice rose over the aisle: 'Oooh, Tom, come look at this onesie. It has duckies!'

Tom shrugged and Louisa smiled at him.

'Everyone knows better than to argue with a pregnant woman,' she said.

The perfect business, Louisa's husband Wade had said of the baby store. Irony of the whole thing: they never had children. It was his idea not to procreate.

'Works for me,' she had said. When they tied the knot she was 34 and running a frozen yogurt franchise. He was 32 and worked in real estate. He came from a different world, slicker and more appearance conscious, and she did her best to fit in. At the nightclub where they met – Lazers – she marvelled that he had chosen her at all. She was there on a hen's night, and they all had silly tiaras and plastic penis cups. He appeared behind her on the dance floor just before closing time – they were playing Europe's song "The Final Countdown", and when he asked her if she wanted to come to his place for a night cap she said she couldn't ditch her friends. He gave her his phone and she typed in her number.

She truly did not expect him to call. But when he did things just slotted into place. Their first date was to *The Bourne Identity* – a film she would never have otherwise seen but it wasn't terrible. It took the pain of decision making away, coasting along beside him. And she no longer worried about making the wrong call.

On their fifth date Wade suggested they move in together. They were both living in one-bedders, alone, and he thought they could maximise their rental outlay. She moved into his place by the beach in Maroubra. Louisa had never lived with a man and was surprised to find that Wade spent more time on his appearance than she did, shaving his entire body every time he had a shower. He took twice as long to get ready when they went out. He had other habits which annoyed her: the way he clipped his toenails at the kitchen table but complained if she left a dirty mug in the sink. He was never very nice to her mum: he called her 'the old bra-burner' because she lived in Glebe and had taught women's studies at uni. But he was so handsome that sometimes Louisa snapped a photo of him sleeping. Yes, Louisa agreed, they did not have time for children. They loved their holidays, their day drinking, nights out and late-waking weekends. At their wedding, he chose her dress and took charge of the gift registry. She worried that asking for money to fund their honeymoon was tacky, but he said it was 'the new normal'. They took out a loan to buy the Maroubra unit. When Louisa's two accidental pregnancies became early miscarriages, she never told Wade. She had thought she was too old to fall pregnant easily, and the miscarriages proved her right.

Now babies were her income and the bane of her existence. The froyo trend was on the downturn, Wade had insisted. Going forward, if they were going to have dairy, people wanted to treat themselves: freak shakes and pick-your-own flavour ice cream sandwiches.

'Frozen desserts are fickle,' he said. But people would always keep having kids. Snot smeared ones who run through the shop, grabbing rattles and jamming their fat fingers in stroller mechanisms, screaming. Older ones who whinge for Toy World, Game Stop and ice creams. But most of all babies: squirming, red, squealing things, with brown oozing from the ruffles of their nappies and yellow sour milk curdling in the rolls of their fat necks. Here's the bonus: mums and dads were so scared to bring home one of those helpless beasts, all she had to do was tell them that some piece of equipment would make their baby safer, or sleep more, and they lined up, wallets open, not even asking how much.

'It's not rocket science,' Wade said. 'You've got to grab the low-hanging fruit.'

A large part of the baby store business ('the bread and butter,' Wade said) was hiring and fitting car seats. They had two trained fitters who alternated three-day shifts. Good enough blokes, just rough around the edges. Louisa would catch a glimpse of more than she bargained for when she checked on them in the carpark, crouched or doubled over the backseat of an Audi or BMW, yanking straps tight. What dangled in her field of vision was not an

Infantino Tug and Play Mobile Activity Centre. If Wade were still around she could get him to suggest, with a nudge, longer shorts, or the wearing of underpants at work. She could never bring it up. She couldn't bear to think how long the fitters would have given them.

As for the hired seats, Louisa told the girls at coffee on Sundays, you would not believe the condition parents brought them back in. Vomit or faeces she had come to expect, but blood? Cracked plastic casings and cigarette burn holes in the fabric? She'd seen it all. She accumulated these stories, hoarding them for Sunday mornings, because otherwise the girls would shake their heads and cluck over her.

'People these days. Lacking common courtesy,' Bev sighed, flicking her hair over one shoulder and lifting her skim latte to artificially enhanced lips. Louisa failed to mention the security deposit people lost when they brought back damaged seats. She didn't tell the girls it would've been cheaper, in those instances, for parents to have bought the car seat new.

The best was the customer last week – older man, suit and tie, hair loss he'd tried to hide with a number one clipper cut but his scalp all peeling from the sun. Second marriage, Louisa told the girls, she could always pick them. He came in, and what did he ask for?

'Just guess.' She had to drag it out, to make sure they were paying attention.

'He wants to know,' Louisa said, stirring foam residue and undissolved sugar crystals in her cup. 'He wants to know is it safe to turn the baby seat in his Porsche 911 convertible round so the little guy is forward facing. In the front seat. His son is three weeks, but this guy wanted him to face forward, so he could "enjoy the ride".'

They'd all cacked themselves over that one. Then Bev left without even offering to pay for her coffee. Bev didn't have to work; her husband had a plumbing company and never once asked her to do the books. When the others were gone, Louisa went to the pub next door and put $100 in coins through the two-dollar pokies. She lost it all. But for an hour she was consumed by the glib clink and clatter, the flash and blink of the machines.

Tom and Cherise appeared at the register, basket crammed with purchases. There was the Wubba Nub giraffe pacifier, the shark bath spout cover, the fruit pull up reusable swim nappy, the Baby Einstein Ocean Glow sensory shaker. There were baby bow moccasins in red gold, a lemon print one-piece romper and three pairs of ruffled socks so tiny they looked as though they were made for dolls.

As Louisa rang the items up one by one, she noticed Tom watching the total on the register climb skywards. A vein in his neck bulged. For the first time since they entered the shop, Louisa looked down at Cherise's stomach, and was surprised to see nothing where she expected at least a small bump. A light summer frock belted at the waist. Louisa's throat thickened. A memory of cramping, blood clots stringy in the toilet bowl.

It was six months to the day since Wade dumped her on the flight home from a holiday in Cairns. Just after the flight attendant told everyone to put their tray tables up and their seats in an upright position to prepare for landing, Wade told Louisa he had met someone else back in Sydney. A receptionist at the real estate office. It made sense all of the sudden, the work calls late at night, taking his phone to the bathroom. They'd been fucking on the sly. He was strategic, he knew Louisa would never make a scene in public. Was the man sitting beside them in seat 17A listening? It felt as shameful as the affair itself. They caught separate taxis from the airport, Wade went straight to the office. Louisa gave herself two days in bed with a box of cask wine and *The Crown*, which Wade could never bear to watch. On the third day she rang a lawyer.

Blythe was the girlfriend's name. Fucking *Blythe*. Rather than split things in two, Wade got the unit and Louisa got the baby shop.

'It's a win-win,' Wade said. Blythe lived in Louisa's former home now, with her fourteen-year-old twin girls and a chihuahua named Chanel. Imagining Wade with twins and a dog was like sticking a finger in her eye.

'Babies certainly aren't cheap,' Cherise said, stroking the inside of Tom's elbow, which was crooked outward, his hand resting on the wallet in his back pocket.

'A little girl?' Louisa asked, though really she should know better than to assume. But the ruffled socks. The lemon romper…

'We don't know yet, I'm hoping for one,' Cherise said, putting her hand on her flat belly. 'I just got the pregnancy test back yesterday. A surprise, really.'

Tom shrugged at this admission, red creeping from his neck to the lobes of his ears. Louisa saw how desperately Cherise wanted this, how she thought it would make everything right between them. There is nothing a baby will fix, she wanted to say, but what did she know? Maybe it would fix them.

Louisa's voice came out shrill, 'Isn't that wonderful. Congratulations!'

The red numbers on the register totalled $227.46.

Tom had retrieved his wallet and slid his credit card across the plastic benchtop. The strangest thing about Wade's absence was that after the fury and grief receded, Louisa had felt relief. The previously unappreciated joy of being on her own. Not shaving her legs. Mugs piling up in the sink.

She picked the credit card up, feeling the raised numbers against her fingertips.

'You know what?' she said. 'I'm going to give you two a discount. Fifteen percent off. I think you will be fan*tastic* parents.'

'Really?' Tom's face grew redder.

Cherise clicked her lime green fingernails on the casing of her phone. 'That is so sweet. Thank you,' she said, blinking fast, confining tears.

Louisa tapped the card and passed the machine to Tom for his PIN. Tom entered the number and bent to kiss Cherise's cheek.

'She's right,' he said, 'we will.'

Louisa felt strangely buzzed the rest of the day. She was surprised by how buoyant the whole store felt, like it was, for once, the right thing. It was, to be honest, not at all what she expected.

Anadyomene

Myles McGuire

After three days in the hotel I started riding the elevators. Tom would leave in the morning, kissing me on the head while I pretended to sleep. Then I'd dress in a t-shirt and jeans and go to the end of the corridor. I'd inspect my smudgy reflection in the identical rectangles, and try to guess which set would chime brightly, split open.

They didn't play music in the elevator. It was mirrored on all sides except the door, so if I wanted I could observe my likeness in the glass. I'd press the button for the lobby, and then the button for the terrace, and on rare occasions I'd sail directly from one to the other. I'd watch the call buttons as it soared and sank, waiting for the numerals to glow, glimmering irises in electronic sockets. The doors would open, on one of the staff or a guest. The staff would keep their eyes lowered while the guests tended to smile in greeting. I'd stopped smiling back when I'd realised my smile had a motionless, puppetlike quality that made people frightened. I knew this because of the mirrors.

When Tom came home in the evening I'd be wearing different clothes. In the afternoon I'd toss my cardigan in the minifridge, then put it on crumpled and cold, so it would look like I'd been out. One day I cut my hand and wrapped it in a bandage so I could tell him about my humiliating saga on the cobblestones. I'd show him some junk I'd bought at the gift shop and say it was from the Palazzo Vecchio, rhapsodise about cathedrals and art galleries, the florid excesses of the Medicis, the reactionary purges of the bonfires. I would interpolate sentences with Italian to remind him, if I wanted, he would never understand me.

Through the window I could see where the red rooves of the city ballooned, like ripe, poisonous fungi after a storm. Behind them the ragged white swell of the Apennines. While I spoke Tom would make negronis and pretend to listen, the way I'd pretend I was asleep in the morning. He'd peel a ribbon of orange and say something like 'Wow, baby. You're like an Italian encyclopedia.' Except he would say it in an Italian accent. En-cyc-olo-pe-dia!

I was supposed to be translating the manual for an exercise machine. The language was simple, but words I understood in isolation would become meaningless when joined with their neighbours. In whole sentences they seemed to swap places with each other. It was as if they were in a tense I'd forgotten. I'd look at the diagrams accompanying the text to see if these clarified how the machine would move, how it would change a person, and all I'd glean were promises of impossible bodies.

In the elevator there was a group of young nuns. They wore running shoes under their habits and spoke excitedly of the tour they would take in the city. Later a woman in a long coat who kept her sunglasses on and did not acknowledge me; and then a bellboy with a pale moustache and a monobrow. Then tourist couples, mostly middle-aged, the outline of wallets visible where they were strapped under their shirts. They'd greet me with Ciaos and Bongiornos, and I would smile and reply, Spero davvero che tu muoia! Then I'd be ashamed and look at the floor.

When Tom returned from work we would drink negronis, then go for dinner at the lobby restaurant. He'd try to convince me we should go into town to eat, but I'd say I was tired, and besides, everything in the city was expensive and touristic. It felt good to say this because it wasn't a lie. When we got back to the room he would kiss me and start to take off my clothes. He'd fling them on the floor and over the sideboard and the television, thinking I found this sexy, maybe it was sexy. Was it? I'd realise I was drunk and crawl onto the bed and lift my arse to him, press my cheek to the mattress. Once I asked him if he would hit me. When he asked what I meant I said it didn't matter.

After we'd finished I'd wait until Tom started to snore. Then I would dress again in jeans, the t-shirt I was starting to consider a uniform. I'd wonder where the hotel laundry was, if I could somehow obtain an actual uniform, become one of the anonymous men liveried in aubergine, who haunted the corridors and elevators and were always going somewhere.

Because it was late I could complete my circuits without interruption, except for the handful of returning lovers, who would hold each other and lean against the mirrors because they were tired from strolling. They would merge with their reflections, like Aristophanes' fabled human arachnids, and when the doors opened for them they'd leave their twins in the mirror, parting painlessly, unaware that without them the other would cease to exist.

A long-haired boy around my age, his shoulders bare beneath his heavy backpack; a short man in a tailored suit; and a giant, in a baggy suit, around whose ear spiralled a little clear piece of plastic; a tweedy dishevelled couple, both reading The New York Times on their smart phones; porters and housekeepers; the nuns. I'd watch them enter the elevator and in their presence I'd exist, I'd remember I had a body, a bladder, a stomach I had neglected to fill. I had olfactory glands, tiny organs which knew the smell of bergamot. I'd move a finger and in the mirror the same finger would move.

I'm worried about you, Tom said to me, at dinner. Is it the translation?

We were down in the restaurant—on my plate little, fleshy apostrophes. Blood had pooled around the cutlets and I felt a surge of disgust, either with the food or with Tom, for the way he called it 'the translation,' as if it were Dante.

You're eating meat, Tom commented.

I'm not really eating, I replied.

He gave me a look, reached out across the table for my hand, held it in his own larger one and said, Darling. I slid out from beneath him and clasped my knife, sliced the cutlet, speared a bit of meat. I moved my lips and my teeth around it, pushed it with my tongue, drank wine when I couldn't swallow.

Have you been to the Uffizi Gallery? he asked, as I emptied the rest of my plate. The Birth of Venus is supposed to be divine.

I stared at him, trying to tell if he was joking, and the way his face fell I could tell that he wasn't.

I went to the gym. It was on the second-highest level, just below the terrace. I wore the same outfit as always, because even if I'd dressed for exercise I wouldn't have known what to do. I was only going to look at the machines to see them controlled by bodies, to see if it was the other way around.

The crackling stalactites of TV sets showed newsreaders who could have been from anywhere in the world, speaking Italian; popstars, who could only have been from space, singing in what must have been English. Compared to the rest of the hotel there was no empty plushness. The carpet was navy and recently cleaned. All along the opposite wall were mirrors. Metal collided with metal, lungs drew air and expelled it in grunts. Like in the elevator there was no music. I walked through the treadmills and weight machines, watching the five or six people operating them, how their faces knit into anguish, then relief, then resolve. They were like the paintings of Sebastian penetrated by arrows, or the Ecstasy of Saint Teresa in Rome; ambiguous affects between torment and abandon. Except they were moving, they were in constant motion, their bodies swinging with the metal arms and pulleys and cables, the same thing over again, their expressions the same tightly described parabola. I was reminded of the torture museum in Venice, its catalogue of contraptions for breaking the body. I couldn't tell whether these machines made pain or deferred it, if the people inside them were making themselves more flesh, or more statue. And I thought of Botticelli's Venus, naked and broken in her fabulous scallop. Because the woman depicted in Venus Anadyomene is not a body. Her stance, the width of her hips and the length of her torso, her legs, are impossible. If she had lived she would have been in agony.

Tom got a migraine. He woke me in the morning, squeezing my shoulder and shaking me, and though I ignored him at first when he started to whimper I flickered my eyes open. He was pale and wet, a big, damp v where his shirt clung to his chest. I managed to get him to gulp an aspirin, put him to bed with the curtains drawn. I draped my t-shirt over his eyes and pretended it didn't look like a shroud.

When he was like this the only thing that could be done for him was to shut out the light. The smallest sound caused him intense pain, vomiting. He never knew how long an episode would last, an hour or the rest of the day, which meant I couldn't stay in the hotel. I didn't want to risk him recovering, going to the terrace for some fresh air, finding me.

I don't know how long I stood in the lobby, looking around at the chandeliers, the curvy birdcage trolleys. I leaned on the wall by a rack of pamphlets for what might have been minutes or hours and read the same descriptions of the same landmarks, the Ponte Vecchio and the Duomo, in English, then in Spanish, then French. I listened to the same conversation unfold at the reception desk until I could have recited it by heart. Benvenuto Signor, Singora. Grazie per aver scelto il nostro albergo per la vostra visita. Come posso essere d'aiuto? Whenever a porter or a concierge approached to offer assistance I blinked and said I didn't understand.

At some point I decided to get on a bus. I could sense I made the staff uneasy, that they were trying to decide whether to phone the police. The bus rattled horribly as we drove, because though the roads were new the bus wasn't, and I found myself nervously waiting for us to spin out over the sleet. I rested my head on the window and watched the hotel shrink until it was featureless, and then the old city rose up, Romanesque columns and Pietraforte, the russet domes somewhere unseen above. Crowds of tourists streamed by open-mouthed. On the old roads the shaking worsened. I gripped the sides of my seat, pressing my eyes closed as the bus twisted and lurched. My lips moved and I didn't know what words they formed, if they belonged to any language or if they were glossolalia, and though I didn't know any prayers it must have looked like I was praying either silently or too quietly to be heard amid the louder noise.

The Loss of a Day

Ann Erskine

One afternoon, half a year before Christmas, Mother realised she was now officially old. She said, 'Don't give me any more knick-knacks, please.' This was spoken snarkily, which made me think she wanted to cause pain. When I looked over her shelves and registered that most of the small *objects* there were gifts from me, I experienced that strange internal squashing of joy that comes from hurt feelings. I was right. Pain was intended and it was meant for me.

The word 'knick-knacks' told me she saw them not as little treasures carrying the weight of my memories, but as worthless fripperies. The little copper vase with its twisted wire flowers I'd sent her from Mexico. The soapstone narwhal, from my venture into Canada's arctic. I turned the copper in my hands, fancying I could hear mariachi music and see the vivid cobalt of Frida Kahlo's house. I stroked the smooth soapstone of the little Inuit-carved narwhal and felt the bone-deep, icy bite of the arctic.

I replaced them and turned to stare out the window.

'*Papa Meilland* is blooming.' I said.

She acknowledged this with a pleased-sounding grunt. The heavily-scented, black-crimson rose was her favourite. Another gift from me.

I kept my back to her, my gaze fixed on the yard. From the oval on the other side of the fence I could hear the sounds of a football game. Excited parental yells. An occasional 'Come ON, son.' Heart-rent groans of disappointment. Under the mandarine tree, rotting fruit dotted the grass. Two doves fluffed themselves in the concrete bird bath, sprinkling droplets shot through with silver light. The air swum with white cabbage moths.

I acknowledged to myself that the garden was Mother's real and only love.

It dawned on me then, that she was not even slightly sentimental. Shouldn't I have been awake to this years ago? What blinkered me? Why had I never seen the sickness in the rose? The signs were always there: the matter-of-fact disposal of pets—dogs and cats that had reached their use-by dates, the constant, gleeful scanning of the daily 'Hatched, Matched and Dispatched' columns in the Sydney Morning Herald, the aloofness displayed when a foot was put wrong by those who believed themselves loved by her.

I knew if I spoke of this revelation to any one of my friends, they'd nod and say something along the lines of: 'Yes. Cold. Hard-hearted. I could have told you, but I knew you'd be hurt.' Strange how others can see what's right in front of your nose when you're utterly blind to it. Like my friend, Annabelle. In court, face blotched and swollen with tears, covered in ugly lacerations and bruises, begging the magistrate to issue a restraining order, yet unable to accept that her husband's jealousy wasn't a sign of abiding love. All the while her friends huddled beside her like a Greek chorus, rolling our eyes and biting our tongues on the words 'We knew. Always.'

Finally, my melancholy still raw and unchecked, I looked round. Mother was already absorbed in the game in full roar on the telly. I eased myself onto the sofa beside her and feigned interest, my head cocked to one side in the manner of a quizzical bird.

'Who's playing?'

Without turning her head she muttered 'I know this bores you silly. You don't need to humour me by pretending to watch.'

She huffed as I picked up the newspaper lying on the little table beside the lounge.

On the screen burly, no-neck men were shoving and elbowing each other. Occasionally one would burst into a run, thighs pumping, hotly pursued until violently brought down with all the grace of a rodeo-steer roped and dragged. The crowd was yelling and Mother was rapt. I quietly folded the paper and tiptoed with it to the kitchen.

I am an only child. My father told me he would have liked a big family but Mother wouldn't be able to cope with the constant disruption of a house full of kids. This had the ring of truth. ' Everything in its place,' was her mantra. The house was always immaculate; never a hair out of place. Mother said differently. Her story was that she'd begged my father to impregnate her again but he had steadfastly refused to relinquish his condoms. Whichever story was true (both, I suspected) there was no pregnancy.

There were times when I'd wished for siblings. When I was little I'd yearned for a baby brother or sister. Later on, I created an imaginary friend. Betty Hognow. Betty had puffy blonde curls that bobbed around her snub little face like pom-poms. She always wore blue, a colour Mother disliked. She was the one who spilt the milk and broke the vase and always walked mud into the house. She'd whisper to me as we sat at the dining table on long Sunday afternoons, after I'd refused my lunch. 'Give it to me. I'll eat it.' I'd hand over the soggy, cold roast lamb in its coating of semi-solid gravy. 'You can tell them you finished it off.'

These days it was just me and Mother. She'd outlived my father and her sisters and the only one still going was her younger brother. We rarely clapped eyes on him. He had a farm up the Valley, running sheep. Uncle Greg looked eerily like a male version of Mother. He had the same piercing blue eyes, the same high forehead and the same fine, straight, brown hair. But there was something cruel and crow-like about his mouth and chin that exposed a violent side that was obscured in Mother's womanly features. He loved teasing. Not the kindly, jolly sort of teasing some of my school friends' fathers used to indulge in – 'Which hand has the chocolate?' 'No not that one.' Laugh. 'Try again,' but a more fierce and frightening kind, that could involve hoisting me up and dangling me over the sheep dip. He belonged to the 'Fee fie fo fum, I smell the blood of a little girl' school.

Mother appeared at the kitchen door.

'Footy's over. How about we go over to the Club?'

We put on our jackets and scarves, exchanged our shoes for boots and headed off. The walk took us a few doors down the street, along an alley between two houses and across the oval. The light was just beginning to fade and the day had taken on a sharp, cold edge. The air was full of wood smoke.

'I thought open fires were frowned on.'

Mother shrugged. 'First I heard of it.'

We ambled across the oval, sidestepping clods of grass littering the pounded earth. As soon as we were on the path into the Club she walked ahead with a strong, even stride. Where was the arthritis? The bad knee?

The Club was a small, rectangular, one-storey, flat-roofed, red-brick building. Exactly like hundreds of other bowling clubs in hundreds of Australian suburbs and country towns. The place was buzzing.

'G'day, Frannie.' The doorman greeted Mother as if he hadn't seen her for years. I knew she'd been there yesterday for Bingo.

She scribbled on the pad and tore off the little slip identifying me as a *bonafide* visitor.

'My daughter.'

I smiled at the man.

'I've heard a lot about you,' he said, and winked.

My smile faded.

'Your mum tells me everything.'

'Oh come on now Jocko. Naughty boy. You'll embarrass the girl.' Mother gave him a coy, sideways look. I could have sworn she was flirting.

An hour, I thought. I can manage an hour. I glanced at my watch.

After Mother cleared a circuit of hellos, a brandy and soda and a few goes on the pokies I prised her away and we strolled home in darkness.

I left her thawing out some soup and a *Beef Stroganoff with Pasta* from a packet.

'Stay. Have a bite to eat.'

My head was throbbing and I was washed with sad, grey tiredness. My warm terrace house was an hour away and I couldn't wait to be there.

'I'd love to. But Morrison will be furious. He'll be starving.'

She rolled her eyes. 'You and that cat.' Her tone wasn't altogether unkind.

A quick, formal hug at the car. 'It was good to see you. Don't leave it too long.'

Before I'd reversed down the drive she was inside and the porch light was switched off.

I was almost home when a traffic light wrenched me out of a haze of reverie. I recalled nothing of the drive; the car was making its own way home. I wasn't thinking straight, my head revolving into meandering thoughts. It was as though a door had eased shut in my face and I was left standing on a bitter, frozen doorstep. Goosebumps broke out and I turned up the heating. Whatever I'd imagined it to be, a dutiful daughter's banal visit to her aging mother, or something else, I was looking at the outside of a gnarled, splintered door. Cicadas rasped in my ears and a chill leaked into my hollowed chest. I had been like this only once before - the day they told me about my father. I was scared of the remorseless ache I knew would follow.

I parked and trudged up the front stairs, shuffled around in my bag for the key and hesitated for only a moment outside the shiny green door with its brass knocker. I turned the key and the door swung open. My heart skipped a little as I took a step into my welcoming hallway. Was it only this morning I'd hurried out to spend the day with Mother?

Morrison greeted me with a demanding 'Meow'. I put my bag on the hall table and he hustled me straight to the kitchen, purring zestily. He wove between my legs, flying his splendid, plumy tail while I opened the can.

Leaving him to his gourmet fish I made my way into the living room. I peeled off my jacket and folded it across the back of the sofa. I sat down to undo my boots and found slippers under a chair. Magazines were stacked in the corner, a pad with scribbled notes beside them. Thursday's flowers - already wilting - sat forlornly on my desk. I turned on the gas heater and slumped on the sofa. I gathered the old granny-square rug around me.

The shelves overflowed, floor to ceiling, with books. The armchair was home to an unruly pile that would have to be repositioned on the floor should someone require a seat. There were no knick-knacks. Nothing was frivolous. Nothing carried my fancies or my imagination or my joys or delights. None of my memories were here. They were all at Mother's. Gathering dust.

The Ibis Bedroom Tree

Zoe Deleuil

At first, it looked like a piece of white sheet, flapping against the cool bitumen of the back laneway. But as Lucy got closer, she saw it was an owl.

The school cleaners arrived, banging their mops and buckets, and it flew away from her, to this laneway. She followed it, avoiding the eyes of the two women.

The white heart-shaped was face turned from her, the wing hanging open, but somehow the creature found the strength to fly a little further, resting against the spring grass that grew along the fence line.

Almost every picture book she'd ever read to Jake had an owl in it. Sometimes, out at night, she would see one on a fence post or low tree, and although it was only a shape, just a little darker than the night behind it, she would feel its wakefulness, its alert eyes on her. Owls should not be seen in laneways in harsh morning sun. It was like seeing a sprite from a fairy tale, turned ordinary and easy to break.

And yet there it was, radiating exhaustion from its dark eyes. Behind her, she saw two crows stalking it. Its panic crept into her, and then it flew away further, to a rooftop, and the shiny black-feathered crows followed.

She went back to her car, eating an orange as she waited for the shopping centre to open. Watching kids stumble into school reminded her of that familiar morning rush, the battle to get Jake fed, combed, out the door and then the stillness, once she'd handed him over and was free.

The supermarket was quiet, with the orderly morning feeling of neatly packed shelves, the smell of fresh baking bread and roast chickens. She got a basket and headed to the magazine racks. She was drawn to the homes magazines most of all. She liked imagining herself in those living rooms where the light was permitted to enter, not spilling in however it liked. The soft beds piled with crisp pillows and the spotless bathrooms, with their deep tubs and artfully hung towels and no one banging on the door while you cleaned yourself up a bit.

She would step into those rooms quietly, respectfully, and scatter rose petals into baths of steamy water, then later, her aches soaked away, she would open the window for fresh air, and settle herself against a square feather pillow, with a china teacup of strong tea, and read a book.

Losing herself in books and magazines was something she had always done, even as a child at the shopping centre on Saturday mornings. While her mum was at the hairdresser or trying on clothes somewhere, she let Lucy roam freely.

Eventually, after a few hours, her mother would find her, and they'd go home. Lucy knew all the safe corners of the shopping centre. The back area of the newsagent, where the shopkeeper didn't mind her reading for a while. The library at the far end of the mall, where her mother would collect her like a final purchase.

It was still so vivid, so easy to slip between now and back then. Funny that she's still lurking in the anonymous safety of shopping centres after all these years.

She turned the page. Here was a renovated cottage. When the couple had first bought it, they had been unable to imagine how it would ever work out. But they were keen renovators, and they embraced the challenge. She read the whole story, smiling, then noticed someone waiting behind her, and moved towards the checkout.

'How are you today?' said Chris.

'Ah, not too bad. Can't complain.'

He raised his eyebrows, then picked up her toothpaste. Looking around with an imperious expression, he dropped it into the packing area, unscanned.

She felt herself blushing and worried that he would get caught. She never said anything, but never went to any other checkout.

Afterwards, she went to the Ladies, and then took her shopping to the car and sat for a while. She spooned some soup into her mouth, thought about hanging pictures on a freshly painted white wall, sweeping pale timber floorboards, and smoothing the quilts in a child's bedroom.

After her mother took her one night and ran away from their father, the two of them moved around, sometimes with sympathetic friends, in and out of rental accommodation that got more expensive with every passing year. Some of her mother's boyfriends were kind and ruffled her hair and bought her bottles of syrupy juice and cheap toys. Others weren't so kind.

Eventually, when she was old enough, she found a boyfriend of her own and did everything she was supposed to. Set up house, had a baby, cooked dinner every night and cleaned up afterwards. It wasn't until Jake was older, maybe five, that she admitted to herself that the home she'd made was not quite right. It wasn't the awkward layout or the lack of a *seamless transition between inside and out.* It was the atmosphere. But she stayed on because the not-homeness of it was familiar, habitable. She was strong enough to tolerate it.

She was used to tension, to problematic boyfriends like the one she'd ended up with. If he were a house in a magazine, he would be one that you fell in love with at first sight, despite *numerous structural issues*.

She would have stuck it out, but Jake had refused to stand for it. For a five-year-old he had no fear. He didn't realise he wasn't allowed to challenge a grown man. If they stayed, he would learn that, and keep learning, and she didn't want to see that knowledge in his eyes. So they had gone one night, once she'd saved up enough money, just like she possibly always knew she would.

For a few years, it was wonderful. The rush of school terms and earning money and steering her son through his days.

But just outside her awareness, the prices crept up, the houses kept getting bulldozed, the rents soared higher. It got harder in tiny increments, and she was suddenly facing fifty and Jake was slipping out the door, and somehow in the years of raising him, she missed the opportunity to secure her own little parcel of real estate.

She'd *left it all on the field*, as the sports commentators liked to declare. But not in a heroic way. Not like a West Coast Eagle.

She realised a woman was peering in at her through her open window.

'Are you OK?'

'I'm fine!'

'You sort of look…' She stared at the tin of soup in Lucy's hand, the spoon. 'Are you… living in your car?'

'Oh no, darling!' Lucy laughed. 'I'm just about to visit my mother, I'm dropping off some stuff at her place. I live in *Nedlands*, for goodness sake!'

She could hear her vowels becoming stretched and refined the longer she spoke, until she sounded exactly like her mother when she said goodbye and walked out of those boutiques, buying nothing, leaving a change room full of clothes for the shop assistant to clean up.

Of course she wasn't homeless. She didn't walk around with a shopping trolley filled with backpacks, like the one she'd come across in a back laneway. That was homeless.

'It's very kind of you to ask though. We should all do that.' She nodded approvingly at the woman, who looked mortified.

Little liar, she heard her mother say.

The car park was starting to fill up now, so she drove to Hyde Park and sat by the lake, which was drying up as all the water was sucked away by the lush lawns and fragile English flowers that grew in the private gardens around here.

This too shall pass. That's what she used to tell herself in the playground when she was wearing stained clothes and always translating the world for Jake. There had been a kind of simple peace in those solvable problems of childhood. Sometimes, watching him sleep, she wished she could keep him forever a four-year-old, or a six-year-old. But she wanted to see the unfolding, too.

And then she did. One day Jake was as tall as her. And instead of rushing to her for comfort when he was upset, he came to her to lay blame. His father would promise some outing, or holiday, and fail to deliver, and because she was the messenger, she got the bill.

One day she saw the father in his face. That same rage. All those years of laughter and playgrounds and Bandaids applied gently to small wounds receded. Then there was bad health, the job gone, the rent unaffordable, and one day she found herself here, hanging around the city fringes, mostly unseen and always harmless.

She walked a lap of the park to get some movement back into her body, slowing down as she passed the playground.

And there they were, scattered under the dark, sinuous roots of the Moreton Bay fig tree. White feathers, bright and clean against the darkness.

A girl was squatting down and picking one up. Seeing Lucy approach her, she held it up wordlessly.

'It's an owl feather,' Lucy told her. 'A beautiful barn owl.'

'What happened to it?'

'Oh, sometimes they lose their feathers,' she said vaguely. She smiled at the girl, remembering that satisfaction of protecting a child from something sad with an easy lie.

'Why?'

The child's mother appeared next to her.

'Look. It's an owl feather,' the child told her.

'Oh. Lovely.' The woman didn't sound convinced as she gave Lucy a rueful look.

'Can I take it to kindy?'

'Do you have to?'

'Please?'

'OK. Take it in for news.' She sighed. 'I'm not too keen on feathers. I always think they are diseased.' She combed an eyebrow with her fingernail. 'I think it was one of my mother's theories, actually.'

Lucy smiled. 'Don't they say that some germs are good for you now? That kids are supposed to play in the dirt to build up their immune systems?'

'Something like that. And my mother had some strange theories. It's funny, I always thought I'd understand her once I became a mother myself. But she baffles me more than ever.' She laughed.

'Oh, I know exactly what you mean,' said Lucy, her vocal chords tightening.

Shut up, she heard her mother say. *Don't you talk about me to strangers.*

But she forced herself to continue. 'I wonder about things my mother said all the time. I suppose my son will wonder about me too.'

They stood together for a while, chatting easily, and Lucy thought, as she often did, that she should call Jake. But she didn't want to bother him. And there was always the distraction of the next thing she had to do. Like having a wash in the disabled toilet block before it was locked for the night. And finding a place to park the car, close to the city for safety, but not so close that she would attract the attention of the rangers when they drove around looking for tourists in their campervans.

She said goodbye to the woman, then sat by the lake and watched the ibises settle onto the bare tree on the island. The Ibis Bedroom Tree, she called it when she used to come here with Jake.

One by one they flew in, white and sleepy against the thickening dusk. She imagined herself as one of them, traveling to safety, to the wordless comfort of being around others of her kind.

They have a home, she thought, her mind taking her to that tree, that island. They find shelter where they can. And only sometimes do they get caught.